"This isn't—" Kirstie forced the words out

The balcony, the air, even the birds were still as he asked very quietly, "Why isn't it?"

"This—this preoccupation," she began.

"Quite an interesting euphemism," he said.

The mocking, angry taunt was so accurate and it hurt. Her eyes flashed fire at him. "Would you prefer that I call it a corrosive obsession?" she lashed out, aware from his face that she'd given every bit as much hurt as she had sustained.

"If we sink into this we won't be dealing with issues, we will be ignoring basic problems. Louise—"

She was too wrapped up in her own agitation to notice how silken his voice had gone as he said very quietly, "Ah, yes, Louise."

AMANDA CARPENTER, who wrote her first Harlequin romance when she was nineteen, was raised in South Bend, Indiana, but now lives in England. Amanda endeavors to enhance the quality of her romance novels with original story lines and an individual style. When she's not writing, she pursues her interests in art, music and fashion.

Books by Amanda Carpenter

Don't miss any of our special offers. Write to us at the following address for information on our newest releases.

Harlequin Reader Service
P.O. Box 1397, Buffalo, NY 14240
Canadian address: P.O. Box 603,
Fort Erie, Ont. L2A 5X3

AMANDA CARPENTER

passage of the night

Harlequin Books

TORONTO • NEW YORK • LONDON
AMSTERDAM • PARIS • SYDNEY • HAMBURG
STOCKHOLM • ATHENS • TOKYO • MILAN

Grateful acknowledgment is made to the following for
permission to reprint their copyright material.

Quotation from Friedrich Dürrenmatt
THE PHYSICISTS
translated by James Kirkup,
published by J. Cape, London, 1965
and Grove Press, New York, 1963
All rights reserved
Copyright © 1985 by Diogenes Verlag AG, Zürich
Used by permission

Harlequin Presents first edition August 1991
ISBN 0-373-11384-6

Original hardcover edition published in 1990
by Mills & Boon Limited

PASSAGE OF THE NIGHT

CHAPTER ONE

WHAT a hell of an afternoon it had been.

Francis Grayson shifted his briefcase from one big hand to another to ease aching shoulders. The light in the lift indicated the basement of the car park building an instant before the double doors slid open. That corner of the basement was pretty much deserted, as it was past the rush hour.

He noticed with irritation that construction barriers and orange pylons were up, sectioning off the corner where he had his parking reservation. Apparently the attendants had not seen fit to warn him of the inconvenience. He set down his briefcase and quickly shifted the equipment so that he could get his car through, and made a mental note to call their office on Monday to complain.

Then, with his customary long, arrogant stride, he crossed the yards it took to reach his metallic silver BMW. The underground lights threw orange stripes on the asphalt and created long shadows between the massive concrete pillars. Down here it was hard to remember that the evening outside was still golden and balmy warm.

To have attained the executive director seat at Amalgamated Trust was no mean feat at the age of thirty-five. Based here, in New York, the finance corporation held offices in all the major cities in the States, together with growing concerns in London, Paris, Rome and Tokyo.

Such success suggested a certain amount of good

fortune, let alone a driving calculated intelligence. Nevertheless, Francis was no stranger to the kind of day where everything seemed to go wrong. It was just a pity that this Friday had to fall victim to one of those times.

He schooled himself to patience. After all, the working day was finished. Perhaps something could still be salvaged from the evening, despite the fact that his date had cancelled. He had two tickets to the theatre burning a hole in his pocket, and he had promised his twelve-year-old niece Jolaine some time ago that he would take her out. He would give his sister Patricia a call when he got home.

Light footsteps sounded; not quite an echo of his own, for the stride was much shorter. Automatically Francis glanced in their direction in time to see a blonde woman stroll around one of the concrete pillars, slight in jeans and nondescript jacket. He was sure he had never met her before, but something about those large eyes, that greyhound-sleek bone-structure, was familiar. An odd sense of recognition hovered like a bird about to perch on his shoulder, but it proved elusive.

The question had barely registered before he wondered where her car was parked, and then dismissed her presence as irrelevant. He reached the driver's side of his car and set down his briefcase. Then a very odd thing happened.

The woman walked to the opposite side of his car, pointed a gun at him across the roof and said, 'Hello, Francis.'

Even unloaded, the revolver had a disturbing unfamiliar weight. The handle slipped slightly in her sweating palm, and Kirstie tightened her grip until her knuckles were ivory-white.

She wasn't sure why Francis Grayson had surprised her. He wasn't exactly what one would expect to find on the glossy cover of a magazine. Or perhaps he was. No smooth good looks here, but the way he had moved through the basement car park had awakened an irrational, primitive apprehension inside her.

He did not walk; he prowled. His fluid body was woven with a tight, animalistic grace that paid mere lip-service to the civilised world. The aggressive jut of those broad, rolling shoulders, the casual swing of the slim hips, those long, distance-eating swift legs—all spoke of an integral, inherent power only tempered by the laugh-lines by his mouth, the long, sensitive fingers. There was an all-encompassing masculinity that surrounded him like a physical scent, and Kirstie's brows drew together in a painful frown.

His face, his powerful body, those beautiful hands— everything about him had gone into a waiting stillness when she had appeared on the other side with the gun. He said almost casually, his emerald eyes on the gun, 'I don't suppose it would do any good to point out that you are making a big mistake.'

Involuntary images crashed through her memory: her agonising over the difficult decision, the sleeplessness, the anxiety, the heart-stopping point when she had walked towards this dangerous man. From the moment he had seen her, it had been too late and they both knew it. She said almost gently, her grey eyes dark, 'No, it wouldn't.'

Several years ago, Francis Grayson had made quite a name for himself playing football for the University of Notre Dame. He had been one of the nation's leading sports figures and could have made his fortune

as a professional quarterback, had he so chosen.
Kirstie had seen film clips of the old games. His speed
had a shocking elegance; the inherent threat she had
witnessed from the moment she first laid eyes on him
in the basement was no illusion, and, even with the car
between them and the empty threat of the gun, she felt
exposed, made vulnerable by the very self-containment
with which he looked down the barrel of the gun into
her eyes.

Oh, God, she didn't dare underestimate him.

He shifted.

'Stop!' she cried, throwing herself back three steps
in panic. Francis froze again. Their eyes clashed; she
felt the impact shudder through her right down to the
ground, and knew by his tight, savage smile that he
saw just how afraid of him she really was.

'Believe me,' drawled Francis contemptuously, 'I
have no immediate desire to get shot. My wallet is in
my right breast pocket. I will reach for it slowly with
my left hand.'

Kirstie shook her head. 'Never mind your wallet,'
she said tersely. 'Reach instead for your car keys—
slowly. Unlock the back door and open it. Now slide
the keys over to me and step back. Back off!'

He did so, like a wild animal retreating from attack,
checked but unbeaten. His voracious green eyes rav-
aged her appearance as he whispered, 'Do you
honestly think that I will let you get away with this?'

So gently said, so implacably meant. Not a threat,
not even a warning, just a simple question ringing with
devastating truth. She ignored the question as she
began to pull nylon cord from the inside of her jacket.
She had to, for if she thought any more about all the
ramifications of what she did, of how she knew this
man would never forgive, or forget, and how inevitably

she would pay the price for subduing him, she would freeze and it would all be over.

She tossed the length of cord to him and he caught it with an automatic flex of his wrist. 'Make yourself comfortable by sitting in the back seat and tie your ankles together.'

His hard gaze met hers over the intervening roof. Even now he showed no fear, but for an instant Kirstie saw the real man through that tough, calm exterior, and she sucked in a frightened breath. She had never seen such rage or reaction shielded with such utter control behind the mask of his face.

'And if I don't?' he asked, with no more emotion than he would when discussing the weather.

If you don't, I am lost, she thought, and directed the gun with meticulous precision at his gleaming dark head. 'Then so much for desire.'

After staring for a long moment at her poised, slim figure, at the unwavering grey eyes, in which were equal measures of pain and driven resolution, Francis eased himself into the car, bent, and tied his ankles together deftly, well aware that her sharp stare missed no detail of the act.

It was a major concession. Her shuddering sigh was silently exhaled as she walked around the back of the car. She tossed through the open door another item, which glinted steely in the air and chinked heavily as he caught it. Handcuffs. Francis raised expressive eyebrows and waited.

Concession, but again no defeat. She conceived the wildest suspicion that he had agreed to go along with her just to see where it led him, not out of fear, not out of any regard for his safety, and she drove her doubts away with deliberate harshness as she snapped, 'Use them! Arms behind, not in front of you! Well done. We've gone past first base. Pardon me, that was baseball. Should I have said the first kick-off instead?'

As she had intended, the dangerously unpredictable rage in those unique emerald eyes faded to speculation. 'You seem to be a remarkably well-educated thief,' he replied.

Kirstie had lost none of her wariness, for all Francis Grayson's apparent incapacitation. The sight of that big folded body lent itself to a great many images, but not one of helplessness. She kept dividing her attention between him and the direction of the lift doors. Every muscle in her body hurt, she was so tense.

However, she forced it all below the surface as with swift competence she swept his abandoned briefcase up from the ground and tossed it in beside him. 'You persistently misunderstand,' she said, prior to slamming the door shut on him. 'You are not going to be robbed. You are going to be kidnapped.'

Kirstie was very aware of that brilliant gaze dissecting her every movement, assessing threat and possible weakness. She now moved fast, racing to the front of the car where she had previously stashed two blankets and a backpack. Scooping them up, she put everything, plus herself, in the front.

She twisted in the driver's seat to parry the slash of those eyes. The interior of the car was luxurious. It smelled of fresh clean aftershave and finer scents. Though her victim was very quiet, the air around him crackled. By sheer force of presence, he dominated the situation.

Two lines had begun to cut from either side of her delicate nostrils, and the short hair at her temples was darkened with sweat. With a movement as compulsive as it was sneaking, she wiped her mouth.

His attention never wavered; he saw her, damn him

to seven kinds of hell. 'It would be a pity to lose control at this late stage,' he said with hideous softness.

'Pity doesn't come into it,' she attacked back. 'One slip from me and you'd go for my jugular vein.'

His eyes shifted down. Malice glittered bright like gold in the air. 'Such a delectable throat it is, too. Granted, you've done very well so far, but you will slip. And when you go down, you are quite right. I'll be waiting.'

Her moving lips felt stiff, her eyes cold. 'Don't bother warning me, Francis. I know all about you. I won't slip.'

Behind his answering silence, she could feel his mind, dagger-sharp and unkind, working furiously. Quite in control now, her fingers flashed over the fastening of the backpack to draw out a thermos. She opened it and poured some of the liquid into the red lid. The bitter smell of coffee filled the interior of the car. She turned back to Francis and aimed her attack again at his composure. 'Black, no sugar, I believe.'

Most would have noted no reaction to that. Kirstie saw a tiny muscle by his mouth twitch. 'Very well-educated indeed, for someone I've never seen before,' he said thinly. 'What other information have you managed to dig up about me?'

'Oh, you'd be surprised. It has been a very bad day for you, hasn't it, down to your date cancelling tonight? What a shame about those theatre tickets. Getting them on such short notice must have cost you a fortune. I know your favourite meal, how well you ice-skate. I know about the scar on the inside of your left thigh.'

'Who are you?' he gritted. He had whitened as she'd spoken. His eyes were so dilated, they were almost black.

She had wondered when he would get around to that. Kirstie held up the cup. 'We have reached a decision point. Will you drink this coffee?'

'Which bears the convenient drug that I am to swallow blind, and hope it doesn't kill me. And if I don't, do you threaten to shoot my kneecap? How I despise your kind.' His mouth twisted with the bitter words.

Kirstie leaned forward, compelled his gaze to hers and held it unblinkingly. For the first time he was close enough to see that her eyes were expressive like rippling water that reflected every mood of the sky.

'If I were a killer, you'd be dead by now.' The brutal truth of that was self-evident. 'Even you should see that you're worth more alive. I checked the measurement of the sleeping drug three times. I don't want to hurt you,' she said, her eyes very clear. 'But if you don't drink this coffee I shall have to hit you over the head with the butt of my gun. It is your choice. Believe me, the drug is more precise and less painful.'

The soft hairs at the nape of Kirstie's neck rose one by one as she held the drink towards him. Bound he most certainly was, but it became the hardest task of her life to force her hand nearer.

Everything past and present converged on the moment as she waited to see if she had intimidated him enough into believing her. This was the most perilous point of the whole enterprise. If he called her bluff and refused, she didn't know what she would do. Kirstie felt as if she had put her hand into the mouth of an angry dragon. An immeasurable eternity of a second passed.

Then, with the first evidence of grace in their encounter, he lowered his head and drank.

Swallowing blind. God, what she had made him

choose! Francis's eyes focused on her hand holding the cup, and he raised his head. She did not know what he saw in her face, but it changed his drastically.

'You're shaking,' he whispered.

She licked her lips. 'So are you.'

His eyes were the most vivid colour she had ever seen, riveted with sudden awareness. 'Could you have hit me?'

'Rather late to ask, don't you think?' She turned her face away and recapped the thermos.

'What would you really have done if I hadn't complied?' he asked, not letting go.

'Oh, for God's sake!' she snapped, vicious with tension, and she glanced at her watch. The drug should take effect soon.

'"The more human beings proceed by plan, the more effectively they may be hit by accident,"' he quoted.

'You might not have paid for it, but it was a very expensive education,' she retaliated. 'Quotations from *The Physicists* should be as good a way as any.'

This time, however, her tactics did not work. It showed in the quirk of his black eyebrows an instant before he spoke. 'Your first mistake,' he told her, suddenly too tired to bother hiding a weary cynicism. 'After a broken ankle, a twice broken collarbone, torn ligaments and a metal pin in my knee, I paid for that education.'

Kirstie could not help her look of surprise, and, though uttered reluctantly, the question had to come out. 'The pin in your knee—that's why you didn't turn pro?'

His downturned lips mocked her. 'You disappoint me! Why else the scar on my left thigh? "The greater our knowledge increases, the greater our ignorance unfolds."' He had not lost one iota of his muscular control, but he curled down into the back seat, nevertheless, and said, 'I think I'll take that nap now. Drive carefully—I have a fondness for this car.'

Kirstie covered his cramped, sleeping form with the blankets, then ran to shift one of the construction barriers she had stolen in the early hours of the morning to place around that section of the basement. She raced back to the BMW. All her movements were concise, efficient. She had gone through everything over and over again.

But the drug should have taken about ten minutes to work. It had taken almost twenty. As she started the car, her heart was pounding. The car purred out of the space and up the exit ramp. What else had she failed to plan for? What else could backfire?

The worst of it was that, for all that Francis Grayson deserved everything he got, through all the good arguments for what she did, the conviction that undermined her entire purpose was that what she was doing was wrong.

'"The best-laid plans of mice and men,"' she whispered, feeding the parking ticket into the automatic machine. Francis Grayson wasn't the only one who could throw in a quote or two for the occasion.

The whole affair had started just forty-five minutes ago.

Kirstie perched on the edge of a boulder with a fishing-rod in one hand. The line curved out and she contemplated the little red bob in the water thoughtfully. The small mountain lake was clear, unpolluted and very cold. She was well aware of the last from personal experience, for the boulder had doubled as a diving point on occasion.

Fishing that evening, however, was not providing its usual sense of relaxation. She had rammed her brain into high gear for over two days and now was finding that it wouldn't stop, no matter how tired she was.

She'd had to cash in some favours owed to her, but at least the rest of the kidnapping had gone smoothly. She had simply driven through downtown Manhattan with Francis Grayson snoring in the back seat. The BMW was equipped with a car phone, so at a convenient stop light she telephoned ahead to warn her stepgrandfather, Whit, that she was on her way to the New Jersey airstrip.

Philips Aviation was small, but was privately owned and operated by Kirstie's family. The authority of leadership fell on the broad shoulders of her eldest brother Paul, who, at forty, was a stable personality and in many ways held the wisdom of a man far older. He ran the business with an iron hand, and he held an obsession for orderliness and practicality.

Primarily her responsibility in the business consisted of flying wealthy tourists around New York, but she regularly helped with the company's shipping schedule as well. On one occasion, when the police had needed extra manpower, she had helped them carry out a road search for a car involved in a high-speed chase. Normally Kirstie loved working for her brother, and piloting helicopters was a fascinating occupation.

What she would face when she went back, however, was something she dreaded, as she was rapidly gathering a great many black marks against her. White-haired Whit, a loyal old scamp, had prepared the number three helicopter in the north hangar for her, and had stocked it well with groceries. He had not liked doing it, but he had helped her carry Francis to the helicopter and strap him in. They had parked the

BMW inside the hangar and Whit had distracted Paul while Kirstie took off.

Kirstie counted, with a morbid compulsion, all the sins she had committed that day. She had taken the helicopter without permission, for an unspecified length of time. She did not know when she would be back at work. She had lied. She had broken the law. She would shortly be faced with a large, very hung-over, very angry man.

It had been a busy day.

She heaved a sigh, shifted aching shoulders and gave an experimental tug on her fishing-line. Most of the lake was ringed by a tangle of underbrush and trees. Some people might have found the scene God-for-saken. Kirstie had loved it all her life. She knew every tree, shrub, and gorge on that mountain, knew every sound it made.

A dead, dry twig cracked.

With a great effort, she managed not to flinch. There was a tiny rustle, like a breeze through a tree branch. The wind had died over an hour ago. The trees were perfectly still.

Kirstie forced herself to remain seated, making him come to her. Pride wouldn't let her look around. He had stopped perhaps ten yards behind her, and the sensitive skin along her back prickled with tiny needles of apprehension. Never in her life had she been so aware of another person's presence.

He began to move again. She watched a fine tremor quiver down the length of the fishing-line as she cleared her throat and said steadily, the first thing that came to mind, 'I assume you've already been through the cabin?'

There was a hesitation. 'Where the hell are we?' enquired Francis in a deceptively mild voice.

God, he was so furious, so controlled, and the reality of it was worse than all imagining. She could not admit to fear. Kirstie had never cowered before a man in her life, and she wasn't about to start now. With a clearing of her throat, she managed to sound calm as she replied, 'Northern Vermont. This land has been in my family since my great-great-grandfather came over from Ireland. That was the log cabin he built—well, at least most of it is original. There have been additions.'

She was babbling. As she became aware of it, she put a stop to the words flooding out of her mouth and heard another twig crack. He was circling her, blood-thirsty as a wolf, and she nearly spun where she sat to draw up the gun and stave off that inimicable prowl with the threat of violence.

'Where are the others?' From over her right shoulder now came the purr of the man's fury.

Kirstie's head turned sharply to one side in discon-certment. 'What—what do you mean?'

A rustle, a whisper, a mere hint of movement and she struggled to breathe against a tightening constric-tion across her chest. 'You're too small,' murmured the wolf, with hideous reason. 'You couldn't have shifted me two feet, let alone managed to lift me out of the back of the car. Let us indulge in an exercise of logic. Two people, maybe three were needed. Plus money, to hire out the helicopter.'

She hastened to forestall him, appalled at his deduc-tions and the possible consequences to her grandfather, Whit. 'There's no one else involved in this,' she grated harshly, and he moved again. It was enough to make her reach for the gun and turn to face him, on her knees in a wary crouch. Lord, he was closer than she had realised, and, confronted with the dangerous glint of warning in her grey eyes, he froze. 'It's my helicopter and my responsibility. You want to blame someone for the mess you're in, you look at me.'

His carved lips drew back over white teeth in an animalistic parody of a grin. The straight black hair that had been so immaculate in the basement car park now fell over his forehead in an ebony wave. 'I have. Should I be impressed?'

That cut so accurately that she nearly shook her head. No, Francis, there was nothing impressive about this sordid scene, only shame and the unavoidable clash of hate. However, she merely replied, her eyes opened to their very widest, 'That depends on whether you refer to your own performance of this afternoon, or mine. For such a clever man, you were remarkably easy to snare.'

Even from where she knelt, the gun heavy in the clasp of one diminutive hand, she could see how the lean muscle in his cheek leapt in reaction. 'Indeed,' he said, making a mockery of courteous speech. 'Let us give credit where credit is due. Like most people, I tend to treat the wrong side of the barrel of a gun with the utmost caution. How astute of you to realise it. If you wish for a real test of wit, try laying down the weapon and facing me without it.'

The rock was digging into her knees. 'But, Francis,' she protested, as she rose to her feet, his caustic stare following her every move, 'then you would have the unfair advantage. After all, you said it yourself. I'm much too small. Pitted against you, I'd be all but helpless.'

'God help anyone who considered you helpless,' he uttered with unflattering sincerity. He sounded a little disorientated, and frustrated as hell. Kirstie couldn't blame him. She bit her lip, grinding the butt of the gun into her palm as though she could crush out her unwilling sympathy for Francis Grayson as easily.

'Temper, temper,' she tutted mildly.

It was touching a lighted match to a fuse. He exploded with the rumbling growl of a thunder clap. 'I've just awakened after being drugged. I found myself with a pounding headache, in a strange helicopter with a missing radio, miles from anything familiar. I was unbound, there was a bottle of aspirin in the empty seat beside me and a note telling me that I was free to go whenever I liked. I ask you, am I supposed to swallow this farce *calmly*?'

She said with a distinct snap, 'You can swallow it however you like! The nearest town is six days' walk to the south. Backpacks and compasses are in the cupboard under the stairs. If I were you, I'd wait until morning before starting out. Wandering around at night on this mountain can be dangerous, and you're bound to be feeling groggy still.'

'What I want, damn your contrary hide, is an explanation!' he shouted.

It was for this that her conscience would not allow her to leave, but even conscience had its limits. Kirstie sighed and replied with obvious patience, 'That is what I'm here for. Do you like lake trout?'

'What do you mean?'

'This,' she said, indicating the rod by her left foot, 'is a fishing-rod. It is attached to the line in the water, on the end of which is a hook I baited with a worm about twenty minutes ago. Very soon a hungry fish should be paddling along, and——'

'Perhaps you have acquaintances who find you amusing,' he broke in, with harsh sarcasm. 'I assure you I do not! I meant, what did you mean by your first statement?'

Kirstie had her own brand of sarcasm in plenty, and she indulged it by pretending surprise. 'Francis, I would have thought it was obvious when you found yourself mobile and free to leave. The exercise is complete, the kidnapping a success! There are plenty of provisions inside, and the wildlife is so shy that you are quite safe to venture forth weaponless. Surely you have already asked yourself why I've bothered to wait around, instead of heaving you out of the helicopter and flying off again, because I assure you there was no need.'

The evening shadows were deepening rapidly and the temperature dropping, but he had shed his suit-jacket. His white shirt shone out in stark contrast to the profuse greenery behind him. Both the rolled sleeves and his stance, with hands resting casually on those angled hips, appeared to be habitual. His baffled fury did not. She pursed her lips and narrowed her eyes, for it was pretty clear that he wasn't much used to being crossed.

Francis stared at the petite woman in front of him. She held herself so tensely that every line of her body vibrated. Her short blonde hair stood up in untidy peaks. It looked as if she simply hadn't bothered to use a comb that day, or—and this observation was made with the utmost reluctance—as if she had run her fingers repeatedly through her hair, in either worry or terrible doubt.

His hard green stare was sceptical as he scoffed, 'You stayed just to talk? I find that hard to believe.'

She said with undisguised contempt, 'You would. The concept involves a certain sense of responsibility for one's actions, a trait that seems to be distinctly lacking in your own personality.'

Underneath his still present anger, she could see his

mind racing. 'Curiouser and curiouser. You sound as though you hate me,' he commented, almost absent-mindedly as his straight black brows lowered in a frown. 'But I could swear that we've never met.'

Her smile was feral. 'Hate you?' she replied with an angry little laugh. 'I don't grant your existence so great an acknowledgement!'

'You acknowledged it enough to break several laws!' he retorted. As he felt surprisingly unsteady on his feet in the foul aftermath of the drug she had given him, he just sat where he stood and dropped his head into his hands. Kirstie watched, feeling strange. Those long fingers dug into his temples, as if by sheer determination he could force his headache away. 'And, like a fool, here I am trying to make sense out of it! For God's sake, why?'

'Louise Philips.' She dropped the name, like two hard stones, into the conversation and watched the ripples of shock spread out. His head reared back with the force of it. 'She is why.'

'God! No wonder you looked so familiar. You must be her sister. You are, aren't you? I should have seen the resemblance before,' he whispered, staring at her incredulously. 'But that doesn't make any sense! Louise is no reason for what you've done!'

'Isn't she?' Kirstie countered in a swift attack. 'You certainly seem to have a convoluted morality. Should I call it a *convenient* morality? Is there any reason for what you are putting Louise through, other than bloody-minded selfishness? Perhaps you can't grasp concepts like loyalty, consideration, simple kindness, but even you should understand sheer desperation.' Silence greeted that rejoinder, and the line of her mouth grew ugly. To think that she was feeling guilty for what she had done to him. She might as well have

saved herself the effort. Kirstie picked up the rod and
reeled in the line. She said abruptly, 'The explanation
is over with.'

'Over with!' he exclaimed, surging upright. To
Kirstie's overwrought mind, it appeared that he just
kept rising and rising forever, until he stood above
both trees and building in a magnificent tower of rage.
'You haven't even begun to explain yourself!'

She raked him with a steel-claw glance. 'What else
did you expect—an apology? This may come as a great
shock, but I don't have to justify my actions to you!'

'You sure as hell should justify them to somebody!'
he snapped. 'Maybe it would curb that distinctly crim-
inal tendency of yours!'

'And you are so very whitely washed?' she sneered
in retaliation. 'Only the sinless are supposed to cast
the first stone, Francis!'

His eyes flashed emerald fire. 'I am a man, not a
saint. I have never claimed to lead a blameless life, but
at least I've always been inside the law! You're the one
holding the gun in your hand!'

'Just call it self-protection!' she snarled.

He barked out an angry laugh. 'As I recall, that
wasn't the case earlier this afternoon! How is that for
a convenient morality?'

Simmering with fury, not the least of which was
directed at herself, Kirstie turned to stalk back to the
cabin, the fishing-rod slapping against her thigh with
each stride. Francis kept wary pace several feet to the
left of her.

'I did wrong,' she said after a moment, with careful
control, and then turned on him grey eyes that were
ferocious with self-condemnation and antipathy. He
sucked in an audible breath at the sight. 'And I'm not
proud of that. I've never done anything so wrong as

what I've done today! I knew it before I did it, I went ahead and did it anyway, and I would do it again if I had to. Somebody had to stop you. You were tearing her apart!'

'But how? Everything you've said indicates that you feel you have some reason for doing what you're doing, but it isn't apparent to me! Listen to me! Can't you see that we seem to be talking two different realities here?'

She would not let him get to her. Unravelling at the edges, feeling every one of his questions chip away at her control until she felt like turning on him and shrieking like a fishwife, Kirstie clenched her teeth and said nothing.

Goaded by her stony lack of reaction, Francis strode ahead and slapped a hand on to the cabin door, effectively stopping her in her tracks. He turned his face, clenched with concentration, towards her. 'Look at it logically. Life doesn't get as crazy as this.'

'Get away from the door,' she ordered him through gritted teeth.

He held up both hands in a gesture that in anybody else would be conciliatory. 'Just wait a minute,' he said sternly, clamping down his own anger with iron force. Then, as she made a sudden, uncontrolled movement, 'Calm down, all right? All I want you to do is answer one question. Aside from everything else, how is putting me out of action for six or seven days going to keep me from contacting Louise after I get back to New York?'

She ran a suspicious stare down the length of his taut body. 'What is the point of all this?'

He leaned forward a little and she drew back. 'Try to stretch your imagination. Pretend for a moment that I don't know anything.'

Oh, he was good. He was very, very good. He was

the essence of troubled spirit and earnest effort. Kirstie could have felt concern, if she hadn't actually known Francis better. Was it any wonder that Louise had been so taken with him, until the mask had dropped and he had revealed his true colours?

The thought made her smile with grim triumph. 'Clutching at straws now?' she asked, with a gentleness that was no kin to tender feeling. His stare was so intent, it was blinding. The pressure from it made her burst out, 'Look—the pretence isn't going to do you any good. With her wedding a week from tomorrow, and you effectively cut off from civilisation, there isn't a thing you can do to stop it now. Give it up, Francis. Can't you see you've lost?'

A pause. Dusk was settling in fast, lending them the deception of its blackness like a cloak, but she was still quite able to witness his reaction. For the second time that day he showed shock beyond all barriers. He looked as if she'd slapped him. Oh, why did he look as if she'd slapped him? Beyond all reason or determination, Kirstie's heart began an apprehensive pounding.

After a moment, Francis said blankly, 'What wedding?'

CHAPTER TWO

IT WASN'T fair.

Despite all the racing her mind had done just half an hour ago, it refused to work fast enough to handle all the implications of what Francis had just said. When the pieces did begin to fall into place, with a vertiginous sensation that was almost physical, she wished they hadn't.

It was so impossible, it couldn't be true. Francis just stared as she shook her head and laughed angrily, both at her own gullible reaction and at him. 'Oh, no, you don't,' she told him, hardly aware that she was backing away. 'You can't take me that easily. You knew all along that she was getting married.'

So much reaction and emotion packed into the man in such a short space of time made his eyes unreadable. All he said was, quietly, 'I didn't.'

That plain statement sounded damnably honest. She cried out against it. 'Why are you lying?'

'Why would you think I'm lying?' he asked, still in that lethally quiet voice.

'Because nothing else makes sense!' A shiver ran all over her body at his own savage laugh, reminding her that they were all alone miles from anywhere, and all that lay between them was a thin veil of deception.

'Join the club. It is not a nice feeling, is it?'

The tension from the day, her sleepless night, the man in front of her all combined to make Kirstie's composure snap. 'I don't need to stay for this!' With an abrupt violence, she threw down her fishing-rod and whirled towards the helicopter. She wouldn't listen to this man's lies, wouldn't let him ruin her thinking. She would go home, and Francis Grayson could go to hell.

She ran across the thick tangled grass to the wide, flat clearing where the helicopter rested, some forty yards away from the log cabin. Here and there the ground was split and rocky; white pines and red spruces at either end of the clearing flashed past the edges of her vision.

At the helicopter, she scrambled into the pilot's seat and strapped herself in. Her fingers flew over the controls to switch on the night lamps; she knew the machine so well, she did not even bother to look.

Francis stood well to one side, put his hands in his pockets and watched. He was thrown into sudden harsh illumination, but Kirstie spared him only a quick glance as she put the gun in her lap and started the helicopter.

Or, at least, she tried to start the helicopter. The overhead blades did not begin their familiar throbbing. The engine did not even turn over. With a horrible premonition that she was wasting her time, she tried again. 'I don't believe this,' she whispered. Her hands began to shake. She clenched them into fists and drove one into the bubble of glass with bruising force. 'Damn him!'

Francis strolled up beside her. He smiled as she turned to stare at him. 'Leaving me alone in the helicopter,' he said equably, 'was the second mistake you've made.'

'Stay away from me!' she snapped, grabbing the gun and bringing the muzzle of it around to him. 'What did you do to the engine?'

'That would be telling. What are you going to do about it?' Kirstie ground her teeth as she glared at

him. Francis took a deliberate step closer. She shrank
back in her seat and raised the gun higher. Then, his
eyes very light, he asked her once again, 'Could you
really have struck me over the head earlier?'

The moments ticked by. Kirstie knew than that he
had her, completely, for she had run out of bluffs. She
was suddenly very tired and didn't care if he saw or
not. The hand holding the gun lowered until it was
lying in her lap. Her lips twisting wryly, she answered
him with a shake of her blonde head.

Francis walked forward, curiously without any trace
of anger. He reached over and disengaged the gun
from her unresisting fingers with care. It was a point
thirty-eight revolver. He checked it and did not seem
surprised to find it unloaded. Snapping the carriage
back into position, he looked at her and said, 'Now
that we've got that out of the way, we'll sit down and
you can start explaining things.'

Gathering strength from somewhere, Kirstie flipped
off the helicopter's lights and unbuckled her straps. It
was now very dark and the night air was musical with
a multitude of insects. Francis stepped back, and as
she climbed out she had the presence of mind to notice
that the gun had disappeared into his pocket. She
refused to look at him as they walked back to the
cabin, where she bent to retrieve her fishing-rod. Once
indoors, she groped for the light switch and flipped it.

Francis had moved to the centre of the room, turning
as the yellow-hued lights came on. Look at him, she
thought, standing there like that, his black hair tousled,
his shirt unbuttoned at the throat, his face lined with
tiredness but containing, above all else, determination.
She could hardly bear the sight of him, and she turned
away.

Francis's expression flickered at the total rejection

of her movement. Frowning, he fingered the curved metal gun in his pocket as he studied the tense defensiveness of her slim body, the blue shadows of bitter exhaustion that the indirect lighting threw down the side of her face, the way she seemed poised for instant flight.

In the dense silence, Kirstie's quivering, tired muscles tightened once again with an apprehension that was becoming almost unbearable. Then the man behind her shifted, and she exploded into action. She was three steps away and moving fast for the door before she realised that Francis had not moved towards her, but away. She glanced over her shoulder, one hand outstretched to the metal screen door against which large white moths were batting mindlessly.

Hands in pockets, Francis was strolling into the kitchen with as much ease as if he were nothing more than an invited guest on holiday. Kirstie hesitated, breathing unevenly as she stared at his broad back. He disappeared around the corner, and almost immediately she heard the commonplace sound of cupboards and refrigerator door opening and shutting.

She was drawn to the noise like the moths were drawn to the light. Footsteps dragging, she peered stealthily around the corner to find Francis Grayson in the mundane act of making a sandwich.

Of course he would be hungry, after working hard all day. She was too, if she were to be honest, growlingly so in her slim midsection that tweaked with sharp, reproachful pangs when she laid eyes on the food she'd put away earlier.

She nearly leaped out of her skin when, without looking up, Francis said mildly, 'I don't suppose you're going to come out from behind there and discuss reason. Madwomen don't, I hear.'

'I can be perfectly reasonable when I want to!' Unfortunately her snapped response wasn't planned. It had just fallen out of her mouth, in angry reaction against how with apparent ease he had regained his former dangerous calm, and afterwards Kirstie could have bitten out her tongue at the way it sounded.

'Ah.' He nodded as if she had confirmed some kind of conclusion he had reached and took another bite of his sandwich. For all the attention he paid her, he might have been talking to the wall. 'I notice some key words there. The question is, of course, whether you want to or not. Are you going to sit down and have a sandwich, or hover around the corner all night?'

Eat supper across the table from him? It would be like breaking bread with the devil. The thought was enough to turn her hunger into nausea. And where was his anger? To all intents and purposes, it seemed to have completely dissipated, but she wasn't enough of a fool to believe that. Kirstie scrutinised what she could see of Francis Grayson, and what she saw had her very worried indeed.

She knew, by his disorientated outburst by the lake, that, for all his formidable command over himself, she had knocked him off balance earlier today. She had threatened him, fooled him, drugged and angered and shocked him, and now there was no evidence of reaction whatsoever. His total control made her go cold all over. That this man was dangerous she hadn't doubted, but she was beginning to appreciate just how dangerous he was, and it put her present position in a distinctly unfavourable light.

What was he planning? What form would his revenge on her take? How would she make her pay for what she had done to him?

He had given her two choices: stay where she was or

confront him. She wouldn't hover, and she didn't have
the courage to face whatever lay underneath this
present façade. There was a third alternative, and after
a moment of consideration Kirstie took it. Without a
word she walked into the main bedroom and, though
it seemed such a flimsy defence, she locked the door
behind her. Then she forced her tired body over to the
dresser, shook out a pair of sheets and quickly made
the bed.

Her sister had been right about the man. Kirstie
should never have entertained even that one moment
of terrible doubt. She could just imagine what he had
been like with Louise, persecuting and suffocating her,
manipulating her into going out with him and hammering at her to call off her wedding with Neil. Louise was
too gentle. She didn't know how to handle men like
Francis Grayson.

Kirstie was honest enough with herself to know that
she, too, didn't know how to handle Francis Grayson.
He had taken control ever since setting foot on the
mountain, and he was calling all the shots. He acted as
if he was the original irresistible force. She punched a
pillow violently into a linen case. Well, he might be
able to direct the action in this scenario, she thought
grimly, but she was holding the trump card, because
today he had met an immovable object.

Whenever that happened, there was bound to be
trouble.

With a chill premonition, she looked back on her
life. How uncomplicated her past seemed, in the light
of this battle of wills that could destroy everything. She
felt, as she had never felt before, as if she was saying
goodbye to the sunny, madcap teenager she had been,
the cheeky prankster secure in the knowledge that, no
matter what she did to the various members of her

tolerant family, she would always have their affection and support.

As a quieter, more restrained adult, she had returned that loyalty to her family threefold. People were either on the inside or the outside of Kirstie's invisible circle, and rarely did they cross the line. But those on the inside, oh, she loved them all; they were hers in the truest, most unpossessive light, to cherish and protect them as much as she could from the sadder reality the adult in her discovered in the world.

But what price would she pay now for that fierce protective instinct that was as natural to, as inseparable from her as breathing? What would it cost the immovable object to hold firm? Her self-respect was already on the line. She thought of her brother Paul, her grandfather Whit. She thought of Christian, of Louise, and hoped with all her heart that the price would not include their respect for her as well.

Francis's head had lifted at the sound of Kirstie's retreat, and he listened to the sound of the bedroom door closing, the bolt of the lock shooting home. He sat there for some time, thinking, and then he calmly made himself another sandwich.

Morning had appeared with full glorious orchestration right across her closed eyelids. Kirstie groaned in real pain and squinted at the source of warm, blinding light. The sun had just topped the trees outside and was shining through curtains she had neglected to shut last night.

After staggering upright to shake them closed, she fell back into bed, but the damage was already done. She was awake, and her mind had already started to run around the problems facing her. They seemed to fall into two categories: the immediate, and the ones facing her when she got home. Since she couldn't do anything about what was waiting for her back in New Jersey, she thrust it out of her mind and concentrated on the present.

On the good side was the fact that she had successfully managed to transplant Francis Grayson and immobilise him for the crucial period before Louise's wedding. However, he had managed to immobilise her in the process, and that was terrible.

She did have control over communications, as she had hidden the helicopter radio, but he had control over the helicopter. It was conceivable that she could sneak away from the cabin to radio for help, but she wouldn't be able to describe what was wrong with the aircraft. Kirstie did not have a mind that could grasp mechanics well.

That meant Whit or some other mechanic would have to make the six-day trek to check out the machine. She could knock two days off that if they used either horses or a cross-country Jeep, so that would be four days. If they couldn't fix it on the spot, there would have to be another round trip for parts, since the heliport on the mountain was literally the only clear place to land for miles. She scowled furiously. Stealing the helicopter for a day or two was a crime of a certain calibre. But half a month lost in manpower and equipment would be enough to finish her off as far as her brother Paul was concerned.

All this, of course, was contingent on getting away from Francis Grayson so that she could use the radio in private. And even the most optimistic train of thought meant that she too would be missing her sister's wedding. The hurt and uproar that would cause made her cringe.

Kirstie's heartbeat began to accelerate as she gradually became more agitated. She buried her head under her pillow in instinctive denial against it. The sheets smelled like the pine dresser, clean and tangy.

She was stuck in an impossible situation. Either she accepted the consequences of acting without Francis's co-operation, which was unthinkable, or she would try to strike a deal with him in return for mobilisation of the helicopter. He would want immediate transportation back to New York, which was the one thing she couldn't give him. That just brought her full circle.

The truth was, she didn't have a clue what to expect next. Louise's description was the only definition she had of Francis Grayson, and social normality had been stripped away. God only knew what he would do outside the restraint of his life and ties in New York.

He could be capable of anything.

Forty minutes later, after a dash to the bathroom for a stealthy shower, Kirstie dressed in shorts and a light blouse, gritted her teeth and marched outside. In the face of whatever that man chose to hurl at her, she would indeed be reasonable and rational. She would refuse to let the situation get her down. Above all, she would refuse to let *him* get at her. No matter what.

All her grim preoccupation fell away in the face of what was outside.

Francis was at the wood-pile, at one end of the clearing. He was chopping wood. The rhythm of it echoed in sharp reports off the lake. The Vermont sun beat down on his black head, making it shine, and rivulets of sweat slithered down his naked torso. The helicopter sat, gleaming pristine and silent, not twenty yards away from him, and the door of the cabin was in plain sight. Already there was a sizeable pile of split logs beside him, yet he still reached for another one to set on the scarred oak stump.

Kirstie let out a long breath, only then realising that she had held it in anxious anticipation as she'd left the sanctuary of her bedroom. The sound of the cabin door shutting had attracted his attention. With the axe held poised negligently in one hand, his sleek head turned to her, he looked as if he considered the point between her two shoulders a favourable spot in which to bury the blade. It was an aggressive pose, saturated with sheer male beauty. Kirstie frowned at her reaction to it before walking around the corner of the cabin.

The sound of running footsteps dogged her. She set her teeth in furious impatience at the way her pulse went crazy. Francis appeared around the corner, jogging lightly, one of Paul's spare T-shirts pulled on in haste.

'Where are you going?' he asked.

'Nowhere with you,' she told him tightly.

He pulled to a graceful stop. The hot sun lent an odd golden tint to his green eyes. It didn't seem quite human. She shook her head and backed away skittishly. 'If you continue to grind your teeth like that you'll have problems later on in life,' he admonished, holding his two great arms across that barrel chest. Her eyes riveted themselves on the amount of muscle, so casually bunched. 'You wouldn't be thinking about using that helicopter radio without me, would you?'

'I don't need the radio.' She sent him a small, unfriendly smile and turned away only to stop with her hands clenched at her sides when he fell into stride beside her. 'Stop following me. I am going for a peaceful walk. You can't come.'

'More to the point, can you stop me?' he replied lightly, sliding his gaze down the shape of her bare legs. Still sweating from the heat of his earlier exertion, Francis's chest heaved once. The T-shirt clung to his damp skin in a maddening fashion.

The thin control Kirstie had over herself stretched and broke. She breathed deep once, fast, and burst out, 'I can sure as hell not go, you rotten bastard!'

'Why do you persist in seeing me as the villain of the piece?' he demanded, his expression changing drastically. 'I don't have to take this from you! I'm the injured party here!'

They stared at each other, and Kirstie could see a degree of her own amazement reflected in Francis's eyes. So neither of them had the control they would have wished for. Unable to think of anything to say to him, she just turned and started to walk away. One of his heavy hands curled around her shoulder to detain her, and Kirstie shrank from his touch in an instinctive flinch as he made her face him again.

Francis's eyes widened at her unmistakable fear and his hand fell away. He averted his face and sighed. 'Don't you think it's past time we talked?'

Two lines that had not existed a week ago ran from her nostrils to the sides of her mouth. 'Going to try the reasoning tack?' she asked, ignoring her own earlier resolve to stay unresponsive and uninvolved. 'What do we get after that, threats? When all else fails, try a shout or two. But we must give you credit for one thing, mustn't we? Obviously you have an awesome amount of faith in your own powers of persuasion.'

'God, you have a viper's tongue,' he said. If a bystander had observed that his demeanour was bleak, Francis would have denied it. 'Have I ever given you cause to think that I would do you physical harm?'

Her gaze wavered and fell. He had managed by that one question to cut out from underneath her the basic understanding she was operating on. No, he hadn't given her cause, even though she had lain awake until the small hours of the morning listening and waiting for it. 'You gave a good impression of it in New York,' she muttered, but even she knew the retaliation was weak.

'I think I had good cause, don't you?' he said tightly. 'I'm calling a truce, damn you.'

Kirstie threw back her head in surprise. The look in Francis's eyes baffled her. She said, 'I didn't ask for it.'

'No, but I'm offering it, which is more than you deserve,' he told her, the tone of his voice harsh and flat. 'Isn't it about time we thrashed out the reasons for your lunatic actions? Did Louise put you up to it?'

'Louise——' she made an abrupt gesture, then sat on the ground suddenly as though her legs had collapsed '——Louise doesn't know about this.'

He seemed impossibly tall from her position. The sun cast his face into deep shadow and blinded her when she looked up at him. 'I don't think that quite answers my question,' he said at last.

'No?' She spread her fingers into the grass, thin, delicate sculptures of bone and sinew, child-sized, and then she began to search for a four-leaf clover.

Silence for several minutes. The warmth of the day was inevitably mollifying, and by some inner radar she knew that the tension had gone out from Francis's body. She began to forget that he studied her closely, watched her every movement.

Then he said, 'Kirstie.'

Every nerve inside her leaped with the shock of hearing his voice shape her name. It was electric, intimate; it felt as though he had pulled her heart out of her body. Her heated face jerked upwards towards him and she felt again that inexplicable fear.

'That's your name. Isn't it?' He sat beside her, cross-legged, his denim-covered knee a good two feet from her own. She had no doubt that the distance had been carefully calculated.

Her fingers smoothed the grass where she had parted it, over and over. 'Yes.'

'Louise used to talk about you from time to time when we were in college. Last time I heard, you had skinned knees and braids and were the terror of the family.'

'That was thirteen years ago,' she reminded him drily.

'At least you've lost the braids,' he shot back without a second's hesitation. Her laugh, clear and bubbling, surprised them both. She concentrated on pulling out clumps of grass and made a pile in front of her. Francis kept his eyes on her fingers as she sifted through it. He said quietly, 'You have no right to do what you're doing.'

Her face hardened and those grey eyes blazed. She turned the full extent of her outrage on to him. 'Don't you talk to me about rights! You change your own despicable behaviour and then maybe you'll have something to say about rights!'

He faced her attack and absorbed it. No anger answered her. Confused and upset, she subsided and stared at his oddly still face.

'Apparently you have made your character assessment of me second-hand,' he said in a flat, dispassionate staccato that had more power than any emotional outburst to reach through all her bristly defences. 'But I can only speak from first-hand experience. Isn't what you're doing the same as what you condemn me for? You accuse me of trying to coerce Louise, but you had the temerity to force my actions yesterday afternoon.

Even now everything I do stems from it. Yet you are acting with justification, whereas I am a monster.'

He couldn't have hurt her more, for he struck at the very heart of her own doubts and worries. Her grey gaze turned inwards, reflecting all too clearly her own bitter upheaval. With a curiously blind gesture, she said, just as quietly, 'You know I never denied that what I did was wrong. There may not be much of a difference between what we both have done, but there is a difference. What you were doing caused ripples that touched a lot of people as they grew greater. I've simply tried to restrain you, so that the ripples affect only you and me and the damage is contained.'

He didn't reply to that. Instead, he asked the last question that she would have expected him to ask. 'Is her fiancé a good man?'

'Neil is a kind, decent, honourable person,' she replied. 'He doesn't deserve what's happened, nor does either his family or mine.'

She sensed rather than saw the words drop into his mind, and without his telling her she could see that they wounded him deeply, all the more because she too spoke without anger now, without attack.

He gave a cynical and tired nod, as if in confirmation, but of what, she couldn't tell. 'Do you honestly think he would thank you for what you did?' asked Francis. 'Most men I know would want to fight for the woman they love. Yet you didn't even give him a chance.'

She flinched visibly. 'You talk about it as though there were honour in that kind of fight.'

That green gaze held hers. 'Isn't there?'

'Then why didn't you fight with honour?' she cried. 'What you did was underhand, and domineering, and bears absolutely no resemblance to a chivalrous battle for the lady's affections! Don't you see that if you had approached this with any kind of integrity I wouldn't have come near the situation? Why, Francis? Was it an ego trip, or a trip down memory lane?'

Francis turned his face away and ran his fingers through his raven hair. Then he leaned his head into his hand, propped his elbow on one raised knee and just stayed there for long seconds. 'I don't know,' he said reluctantly. 'I just don't know any more. University was fun. Even the bitter winters. Something crazy was always on and stupid pranks were being pulled. Louise and I went to as many movies as my budget could afford. I've been thinking about a lot of things recently, and one of those things was Louise, so I looked her up. I wondered how she was getting on, and whether she was happy or not.'

Kirstie stared at him, working hard to piece together the images he gave her. There was no reason to doubt his explanation for getting in contact with Louise; it didn't conflict with anything her sister had told her, and it made sense, but what troubled her was that his motive stemmed from a sense of comradeship and shared experience, and a caring that was totally at odds with his hard-bitten, relentless pursuit of Louise.

'If that was the case,' she asked slowly, watching his every flicker of expression, 'why couldn't you just leave it at that?'

He looked at her, clear-eyed. 'As far as I was concerned, I had.'

'Louise said you were so ruthless that when she tried to tell you about her forthcoming marriage you wouldn't even listen. I listened,' Kirstie said painfully. 'She cried about it, and I listened all night long.'

'I can be ruthless,' he replied at last, and he did not sound proud of the fact. 'I can push, and cut and scheme, and have done on more than one occasion. I wouldn't be where I am if I couldn't, where for every success there's a criticism, and where, for every strength, my rivals are looking for a weakness. But I never thought to turn that ruthlessness on her. I didn't want to. I never tried.

'Louise didn't tell me,' Francis said, lifting his head to meet her gaze. 'There was never a mention of a fiancé. There was no talk of a wedding. The second time we met, she had called me. We ate dinner that night at a restaurant she recommended.'

Kirstie started to shake her head. It was horrible. In her naïveté she had thought him capable of physical violence, but the reality was worse. Looking into his candid gaze and hearing what he said was much, much worse.

'You don't understand,' she said, fighting back tears, she didn't know, fighting back something. He stopped and looked at her. 'This isn't doing any good. Why wouldn't Louise tell me the truth?'

Like a cloud passing over the sun, an incredible pain darkened his face. 'Why, indeed?' said Francis.

His brief expression of hurt was the final straw. Like salt in a wound, it stung her into crying out, 'Either you or Louise is lying. And *you* have to be lying. Don't you see? You have to be lying.'

She thrust herself off the ground. He just stared at her, head thrown back, an odd glint in his eyes. She didn't want to know what it was she saw there, shining green.

'Kirstie,' he said, and it was spoken with gentleness.

'Don't talk to me.' Her mouth trembled around the words. What more could he say? How much more damage could he try to do? She put both hands in front

of her as if to ward him off, then ran back to the cabin
and locked herself in her room.

She had forgotten to make the bed. She leaned
against the door as she stared at the rumpled blankets
and sheets, her ears straining to pick up some hint of
pursuit, but there was nothing.

Left alone, Kirstie dug the heels of her hands into
both eyes with such fierceness that she saw blood-red
stars. Outside her window a bird burst into a piercing
warble seconds before launching into flight, frightened
no doubt by the scrabblings of some small animal in
the underbrush.

She recalled everything she could about Francis's
true nature, repeating the litany religiously as if she
could somehow shore up the shaken foundations of
her faith.

Francis Grayson was unconcerned for the feelings of
fellow human beings. Supremely selfish, he was ruthless by his own admission, domineering and unscrupulous, everything she despised in a man. He rode
roughshod over anyone who dared to get in his way.
All this she had come to believe of him.

But unfeigned pain was in his voice when he talked
of Louise. And patience was what he had needed to
overcome his anger and her defences, to attempt a
conversation to begin with. Granted, he had defended
his position, but she would have done the same. He
had used reason, logic, the assumption of common
decency, but he had never once, not even in the height
of his outrage, attempted to overtly force her into
returning him to New York. She had indeed seen no
sign of the monster that weekend, just a baffled and
infuriated man trying to cope as best he could with a
problem he didn't choose.

Where did that fit in with all the rest?

It didn't. It couldn't; the images were too incompatible. Francis had been right when he had talked of two realities yesterday.

The memory of Louise rose in Kirstie's mind, those lovely blue eyes swollen and red from crying, the desperation in her clutching hands, the misery in her face. It had been such a simple lie.

Only Louise could have thought she could get away with it. She had said she was going out with her fiancé, Neil, that evening, But Kirstie was the one who had answered the phone much later. And it was Kirstie who, out of kindness and concern, had lied to Neil when he'd asked if he could speak to Louise. When she had faced her sister with the subterfuge, Louise had fallen to pieces.

'Francis won't leave me alone,' her sister had sobbed. 'I know him—I know what he's like. He never has tolerated opposition. What he wants, he takes, and now he's decided after all these years that he wants me. Promise me you won't say anything! Can you imagine what it would do to Neil if he found out? It would destroy him! But I had to see Francis again, to try to reason with him! What will I do, Kirstie? What will I do?'

The question echoed in her mind and wouldn't stop, along with her own reassuring reply. 'Don't worry about it any more, Louise,' she had said gently. 'You just concentrate on enjoying your wedding on Saturday and the honeymoon afterwards. Nobody will find out about Francis Grayson. I will see to that.'

Now Kirstie held up a mental mirror and saw in that statement a reflection of her own unthinking arrogance. Now she was dealing with confusion too. The Vermont cabin had always been a refuge from the world, but she had brought in the enemy and sacrificed the serenity of the place to a private war.

And she had never felt so alone. There was no one she could talk to of her confusion and doubts, no friend in front of whom she could lay her problems and have them dealt with with sympathetic objectivity; only Francis Grayson, who could twist every situation to his own advantage, who played with words and destroyed her peace of mind.

With a sigh, she determined to thrust her doubts about him aside. After all, there had to be some attractive aspects to the man, to make Louise fall for him thirteen years before. He must know how to use them to the fullest extent. It was a very, very clever man who showed her his best in order to get from her what he wanted. What she was seeing was nothing more than pretty packaging wrapped around a soiled core.

'Fine feathers do not make a tasty bird,' she said aloud to a bluejay that had just perched outside in the bush. As if in answer, it shook its gaudy head, cawed raucously and flew away.

Pity, she thought belatedly. That was what had been in Francis's eyes.

CHAPTER THREE

FRANCIS was at it again. Chopping wood.

It was a beautiful Sunday afternoon, the kind which, out in normality, people shared with their children and pets. The parks in New York would be full with ice-cream vendors and hot-dog stands. On a day like today at home, Kirstie would be washing her car or helping Louise pack the rest of her things preparatory to moving out of the small house which had once been their parents' and which they now shared.

Francis showed absolutely no intention of leaving, which she thought was very unreasonable of him. The rest of Saturday had been hideously uneventful. Since there was always a large stack of paperbacks kept at the cabin, which was updated whenever any visiting member of the family thought about replenishing the stock, she had read throughout the afternoon. And Francis had chopped wood.

In spite of the sinuous flow of muscles that pro-claimed him innately athletic, he was awkward about it. And that evening, when Kirstie had shouted brus-quely out of the door that dinner was ready, he had handled his silverware with evident clumsiness, so he must be bearing a good many blisters.

Kirstie twisted restlessly on to her stomach on the rather shabby, conmfortable settee. Her thoughts wouldn't let her settle to any one thing, and attempting to read the dog-eared thriller she clutched in one hand was quite useless.

There were two kinds of men in Kirstie's life. Her

grandfather, Whit, her brothers Paul and Christian—
even Neil fitted into the solid, predictable mould. She
knew what to expect from the men in her family, knew
them so well she could even rely on their weak points.
They were comforting in their stability, and their
loyalty to both family and close associates was without
doubt.

Once she had learned through personal experience
about the other kind of men, they too became predictable. They had an innate falsehood built into their
make-up, one so pervasive it could take months to
discover what was really truth and what wasn't, for
they lied even to themselves.

They presented themselves so often in the light of
what they would like to be, not how they really were.
They built their own self-image up so assiduously that
the fiction became solidified into memory.

Her first serious relationship was with one such man.
She had fallen so deeply in love with the way he had
portrayed himself that the breakdown of her faith and
trust in him was a slow crumbling agony. Each little lie
was a betrayal, each promise hollow. He would agree
to something on principle and believe himself to be
honest, but when she would confront him with the full
force of her open candour he couldn't cope. He
couldn't meet her face to face, and every time would
back away.

Kirstie had come to view men of that calibre with a
mixture of exasperation and compassion, for she had
no doubt that what they did stemmed from insecurity,
the need to be respected, the need to be loved.

But now she was faced with a quandary, for Francis
did not fit into either category. If Louise was right, he
was capable of a deception that went far beyond mere
self-protection. It was a disturbing possibility, for the

detail and consistency of his lies hinted at a love of michief for mischief's sake. She feared the man might be totally heartless.

If—just for the sake of argument—her sister was wrong, everything Francis had done might indicate that he was indeed willing to be honest and open. He certainly seemed to refuse to paint himself into a romantic self-delusion. He could discuss his faults with a ruthless objectivity but he was so damned unpredictable, Kirstie never could tell for certain which way the man would jump.

And the sneaking suspicion, fuelled by the accuracy of his argument from yesterday's conversation, crept up on her that somewhere along the line he had managed to get streets ahead of her. She thought she was being manipulated. She hated to think she was being read like a book. And above all she dreaded finding that she was completely wrong about him, for it cast all sorts of unsavoury speculation on her sister, whom she had loved since early childhood.

Every pursuit of thought led to a dead end. There was no way out of the maze, but still she ran, faster and faster until she felt as if she'd gone into a flat spin.

And, throughout it all, Francis just kept chopping. The sound was a bit like listening to a leaky tap. Thunk, thunk, thunk. It drove her crazy with its incessantness, its lack of purpose. There was a minimountain of split wood behind the cabin already, and besides, Francis couldn't be feeling the urge to do any favours, not after yesterday.

Thunk, thunk. . .

Kirstie sat bolt upright. In the sudden silence, lounging supine on the old comfortable settee seemed a horribly vulnerable position in which to be caught. She was just in time, for the sturdy screen door was thrown open and Francis strode in.

He didn't spare her a glance, however. Kirstie's untidy head swivelled to follow his frowning progress down the tiny hall and into the bathroom. The door slammed shut.

She heaved a great sigh, and her eyes travelled back to her book. Something would have to be settled between them, for this silence was unbearable. There weren't any rules, any guidelines one could count on, just this frigid stalemate where one couldn't make a move without the other's consent.

Almost immediately the door to the bathroom swung open again. She looked up as Francis stalked towards the settee and stopped dead in front of her, still wearing that preoccupied, serious frown. Instinctively she knew that this was it, decision time. Evidently he had, by his own route of thinking and priorities, come to the same conclusions she had.

'Got any tweezers?' Francis asked.

'What?' Thrown off balance by the odd request, she blinked owlishly at him.

'I said, have you got any tweezers? I've got a splinter in the heel of my hand, and it hurts like the devil.' Impatience flitted across his face. Irrelevantly she noticed that he was already getting tanned by his two days out in the sun. It suited him, that flush of healthy brown crowning his strong nose and cheekbones, the bare, straight shoulders, the tight ripple of muscle that played like an accordian down the front of his torso.

'Oh, for heaven's sake,' she muttered, as much to herself as to him. She pushed off the settee in one smooth uncoiling move. 'I doubt it, but hold on a minute. Let me check my bedroom.'

She had meant for him to wait in the living-room but, much to the detriment of her composure, he

followed close behind. The knowledge that he was
looking over her shoulder as she entered her small
bedroom and searched the dresser drawers made her
clumsy. As a result, when she turned back to face him,
she was shorter with him than she might otherwise
have been.

'No luck.' Her gaze collided with his, bounced away.
He stood blocking the doorway, with large arms folded
across his bare chest as if he had nowhere else in the
world to go. Kirstie made a tentative movement towards
him as if she would have liked to walk right through him,
or butt him out of the way, but he didn't budge. 'Look,'
she suggested tightly, wild to get him away from her
bedroom, to break that even, emerald stare, 'why don't
you go soak your hand in water, or something?'

He shook his head, without moving, still watching
her. 'Wouldn't work. The splinter's too big.'

'Well, what do you expect me to do about it?' As
soon as she had snapped the question she could see
how inappropriate her testiness was, and those sleek
black brows of his rose in delicate reaction. 'I'm sorry,
ignore that. Why don't you let me have a look at it?
Since I can use both my hands, I might be able to get
at it more easily.'

Silently, like a little boy, he stuck out his hand palm
upwards. Kirstie was forced by her offer of help to step
nearer, but all awareness of his half-clad body faded as
she focused on the raw mess that was his hand.

'Oh, God,' she muttered with a wince. Three large
blisters had formed at the base of his long, dextrous
fingers. Two had already burst, and the third was an
angry, abused red. Without thinking, she curled her
smaller hand around his sturdy wrist. Her fingers could
only come part-way around it. 'Why are you doing this
to yourself?'

His skin was warm, but his voice was not. 'It's called,' said Francis succinctly, 'sublimation. Better to take my frustrations out on the chopping block than to throttle the only helicopter pilot in this neck of the woods.'

Kirstie refused to look up and meet that intent green stare she could feel was boring into the top of her head. 'You could just leave, you know,' she replied, the audible glaciers in her voice expressing her displeasure at his presence.

'What, and miss such a charming house-party?' She hated the mockery in that, and her telltale fingers clenched around his wrist until the bone was a fleshless ivory. His free hand came up, cupping her chin and tilting it up. 'Besides, I don't fancy a six-day walk,' he told her closed, tight face. 'I'd far rather hitch a ride.'

Her grey eyes flashed. 'Don't hedge your bets, Francis. We're a long way from that one.'

His expression never wavered. He just absorbed her aggression as he had ever since they had reached Vermont, and Kirstie felt as if she were throwing herself, body and soul, against the granite side of a mountain. 'That is something I want to talk to you about.'

'You can talk all you like,' she told him, baring her teeth in a humourless smile. His touch on her vulnerable facial skin was unbearable, and she jerked her head away. 'It won't change anything.'

One side of his mouth twisted. 'Don't you think you'd better wait until you hear what I have to say before you make such sweeping statements? I thought better of you than that.'

He thought better of *her*? What new ploy was this? Her own cynicism showed in her face, pulling the precise features into an older, jaded expression that didn't suit their delicacy. 'What a marvellous transition from Friday, when you thought me despicable. And you had sounded so sure of yourself,' she told him. He didn't just look at her. He smiled. 'Do we try to get that splinter out,' she snapped, 'or not?'

He stepped to one side and bowed her ahead of him. Gritting her teeth, she pushed past. She couldn't help but notice how her sleeveless shoulder grazed lightly along his chest. He was warm and smelled of sunshine and sweat.

In the strong kitchen light, she inspected the splinter embedded in Francis's hand. It was indeed a large one, an alien splice through the whorling pattern of his handprint. The area around the puncture had already begun to swell. It must be quite painful, and, unknown to her, Kirstie's forehead wrinkled as she stared at it.

Francis was watching what he could see of her downbent face, and that male gaze grew sharp with conviction. 'You have such a nerve,' he said.

The unexpectedness of it was like an attack. It shot past all her barriers and hit inside, and Kirstie's head snapped up as she took a step back from him in shock. Francis advanced; now he was the aggressor with a new, inexplicable anger, and the recognition of just how big he was barrelled through her all over again. She retreated until her back was pressed against an unyielding kitchen counter, her mind pounding with disconcertment, incomprehension.

'Pain!' Francis drove the word at her, and he thrust his open palm under her nose. 'You don't like it, in anyone! It's written all over your face! How the hell did you pull last Friday off?'

She stared at him, with her eyes huge and dark, a reflection of the conflicting emotions heaving inside.

Quietly she said, 'It wasn't that difficult. You saw what you expected to see.'

'Oh, Kirstie,' he whispered, and the warning in it twisted her own words on her like a knife. Her mouth tightened with the unhappy pain of it, and she jerked his hand down to focus on it with desperate intensity.

'Grit your teeth,' she muttered, and she pinched the flesh surrounding the splinter with the nails of her thumb and forefinger. He emitted a small grunt but otherwise made no protest, and held absolutely still. The splinter wouldn't budge, however, and she had to swab the area with antiseptic and use the gleaming razor-sharp point of the kitchen's paring knife at the point of the puncture with careful precision. When she was finally able to pull the small wooden spear out with her fingernails, she smeared antiseptic over his blisters and wrapped a strip of gauze around the raw areas of both hands.

'Thank you,' he said.

She shrugged, an impatient answer, and stored the first-aid things back in the cupboard where they belonged. In quite a different tone of voice, in a tired tone, Francis said, 'You really hate it when you have to be civil to me, don't you?'

She stopped in the middle of shutting the cupboard door. Sometimes it was so hard to remember that she disliked him; forgetfulness crept in between the pleases and thank-yous, and passing the salt at the dinner table. Somehow in the midst of them he became just a pleasant, personable man.

Again a stab of that unhappy pain. Her lips betrayed her with a tremble as she turned and replied grudgingly, 'Yes. I suppose I do.'

His expression was unreadable in the pause that followed. Then he made a gesture towards her. What

he meant to convey by it she wasn't to know, for she
cut it dead by her own instinctive recoil. They stared
at each other, wondering, troubled, until her own
precarious uncertainty became too much for her. She
turned abruptly and walked out of the kitchen.

She spent the remainder of the afternoon in a huddle
by the lake, her mind a deliberate blank, desperate to
soak up the quietness and serenity of the scene until
finally her tense muscles unravelled and all human
clashing seemed bearable.

At last that afternoon Kirstie managed to catch two
lake trout. Francis appeared from wherever he had
gone while she was in the midst of cleaning and gutting
the fish. She was all too aware of his fascinated
attention as she worked with swift competence, her
nostrils pinched in distaste for the messy job, which
turned to surprise at his quiet chuckle.

She paused and looked at him 'What?'

He was still laughing. 'You have a very expressive
face.'

Standing there. His white grin open. His demeanour
uncomplicated. Kirstie realised that Francis did not
have to work to create this impression of well-being.
His capacity to be at ease with his surroundings and
himself was a wholeness of personality she had not
expected of him, and was another piece of the jigsaw
about him that did not fit.

She scowled her incomprehension and he, perhaps
deliberately, misread it. 'Never mind, you're nearly
done with it. Er—is one of them for my supper as well,
or must I try to catch my own?'

She looked down at the fish. She hadn't had to catch
two. She didn't have to share, and he certainly did not
expect it of her. They weren't even socially obliged to
sit down together at mealtimes. Her scowl deepened.

'Well, I can't eat them both,' she grumbled, 'and it's too late to throw one of them back now.'

Francis smiled. 'While you're busy at that, I'll go see what else we've got for supper. Would you like a salad?'

She was as crazy as he was, to be going along with these courtesies. She sighed and said, 'Might as well.'

The bizarre homeliness lasted through the short meal. Afterwards Francis cleared away the plates and made two cups of instant coffee, adding to hers a dollop of milk without having to ask. He brought it to her as she stared broodingly at the salt- and pepper-shakers, chin propped on hands.

He curled his long body neatly into the chair opposite hers. Then he asked, 'Is your objection confined to me, or does it actually spread to all the employees at Amalgamated Trust?'

That brought her out of her trance. 'Don't be silly,' she exclaimed involuntarily. 'Why would I have anything against them?'

'But you understand that, as executive director, I am responsible for not only them but the thousands of independent investors in Amalgamated.' Francis didn't look at her. His head was bent as he lounged back in the kitchen chair. He had removed the gauze strips and seemed to be studying the spot in his hand where the splinter had been.

Kirstie could sense a logistical trap coming and grew correspondingly wary. 'Go on.'

His eyes flashed to her. 'There will be chaos and panic tomorrow, if I don't show up at the office. If the news of my disappearance leaks to the Press, the damage will be incalculable. Stock prices will plummet, several vital international deals will be disrupted. A lot of other people's money would be lost. Need I go on?'

Kirstie had whitened as Francis spoke. She shook her head, her mouth tight.

He sighed. It rocked her heart. Again, where was the monster? This was simply a careworn man, troubled by his responsibilities. 'How had you expected to avert all this, then?' he asked her quietly. 'How does this fit into your system of values?'

Kirstie was silent for a long moment, her mind whirling. This was what she had failed to plan for. This was where the whole lunatic idea, born of an emotionally charged midnight and planned in haste, fell apart. This was where he caught and held her by logic and common decency. This was where he demanded that she take him back, and she would be unable to refuse him.

Kirstie looked Francis in the eye and unflinchingly turned the blade of her honesty on to herself. 'It doesn't fit,' she said.

He didn't smile in triumph; he didn't home in for the kill. Instead, Francis looked away. 'So you agree that our argument is entirely private?'

That threw her. What was he trying to get at now? She wanted to shout her confusion at him: I get the point, you don't have to use a sledgehammer! But instead she heard herself say, 'Yes.'

'Then,' he said delicately, staring at his hand again, 'I think you should let me use that helicopter radio, so that I can leave a message at the office. As long as they know to cover for me, the associate directors can act in my place until I get back.'

'Let you use the radio?' she exclaimed incredulously.

That brought his head up with a snap. He said in a hard voice, his eyes completely shuttered, 'Yes. You'll have to take my word for it that I won't broadcast the kidnapping. You'll have to trust me that far. After what you did to me on Friday, you owe me that at least. Then you and I will work this out on our own.'

What was he doing? She stared at him as if he were crazy, which, according to all the evidence, he was. He could have made her take him back, but he hadn't. Instead he had demanded the only other alternative, and, until he fixed whatever it was that he had done to the helicopter, she hadn't any choice.

'Right,' she said, still staring at him. 'Fine. I'll go get the radio.'

Francis nodded, leaned his head back and closed his eyes. 'I knew you'd see it my way.'

Kirstie dragged the plastic-covered radio out from under the bush where she had stowed it, absent-mindedly brushed the insects away and carried it back to the cabin. There she sat and listened as Francis, by a series of relayed calls, managed to get a message to one of his associate directors.

Kirstie curled her legs underneath her as she sat in the corner kitchen chair, watching Francis as he leaned back in his own seat, his closed eyes tilted to the ceiling. He held the mike to his mouth while rubbing the back of his neck with the other hand. There was no way she could have guessed his relaxed, tired posture from his crisp voice, or the quick relevance of his replies.

As she watched she realised, rather belatedly, that what she witnessed in Francis was a character trait of long standing, one developed no doubt over years of hard work, pressure, and being pushed to the limits of his endurance. He knew what to conserve and when, and he knew just how to expend the energy with spare economy. Just enough, no less and no more.

The explanation he gave over the radio was sketchy

at best. It hinted at transportation failure on a long-distance weekend trip and that he would be back by the end of the week. When he had finished he adroitly put an end to the conversation in such a way that he could not be asked any awkward questions, then he put the headphones down on the kitchen table and looked up to meet her eyes.

'Surprised that I can actually keep my word about something?' he asked sarcastically. For some reason he looked angry.

Kirstie sighed. The effort to understand what was going on was wearing her out. 'Francis,' she stated with ragged feeling, 'I should know better by now than to be surprised at anything you do.'

With that she gathered up the radio and went outside to install it in the helicopter once again. There wasn't any point in doing anything else. At least that was one rule that had been established today.

The sun was sinking as evidence that they had somehow managed to argue away several hours. Long shadows thrown by the pine trees crept across the grass, and already the night-time symphony of grasshoppers and crickets had begun. Kirstie sprawled across the pilot's seat and struggled to get the bolts at the back of the radio tightened while trying to keep it pinned into its niche with one knee.

She felt it then without any reason. There was no sound, no overt warning, nothing perhaps except for a displacement of air that could have been the wind, but it raised the tiny hairs on the back of her neck so that she lifted her head and looked up at Francis.

She smelled coffee at the same time. His silhouette, black against the last blinding rays, was motionless only a moment as she twisted where she half lay, half sprawled to stare up at him. She winced away from the rose-gold solar knives when he set the cup down on the rubber-matted floor and leaned over her.

'Here, let me hold that,' he said, taking the weight of the radio in one outspread hand so that she could stretch her cramped leg. 'You should have told me you meant to do this now; I would have come out to help.'

He had to lean in from the front passenger seat, and his taut-muscled arm, bare and smelling of fresh-cut wood and sunshine, was a hair's breadth away from wispy blonde hair at the side of her head. Her hand on the tool tightening the bolt slipped, and she banged the knuckles painfully against the metal.

Exclaiming with frustration and pain, she brought the throbbing hand to her mouth to suck on it too briefly before crying out, 'If I'd wanted any help, I would have asked for it!'

'Well, what would you like me to do now?' asked Francis mildly. 'Let go of the thing?'

Kirstie hauled herself sideways, up and away to sit with her back to him, her legs dangling out the side. 'How can you be so reasonable when only ten minutes ago in there you were spoiling for a fight?' she demanded, feeling ridiculously close to tears. She'd lost her tight grip on her confusion and it was threatening to swamp her.

Francis shifted as well. He had a harder time than she in manoeuvring in the confined space, but he did his best to turn to look at her hunched back. 'Yes, well,' he said, 'I had a chance to cool down. I didn't mean to——'

She recoiled as if he had struck her, and his breath caught in his throat. 'Don't——' she whispered '—don't bring me coffee, apologise, be nice. It only makes it worse.'

After a moment his voice came from behind her, as

carefully as if he trod on cut glass. 'Do you want me to
be something that I'm not?'

Through deadened lips she whispered, 'But who are
you?'

'You know something, that is the first time you've
asked me,' replied Francis. 'I could probably tell you.
But then you wouldn't believe me anyway.'

Her heavy head sank down into her hands. She
heard him move carefully, then there was a slight
rhythmic creaking of metal. In no time at all he had
the radio bolted securely into position, and then he
swung himself lightly out of the helicopter without
another word.

She lifted her head and looked around when he left,
watching until he had gone inside and the cabin door
had banged shut. Unexpectedly her eyes filled with
tears that she would have given anything to avoid. Not
for him. Not these. She didn't want to cry over or
because of him.

She didn't pretend to understand it. Oh, no. The
only thing she could lay honest claim to was this
bewilderment that rose so strongly inside her that the
feeling was painful.

She pressed the fleshless backs of her fingers into
her cheeks furiously in an effort to clear her mind.
Somehow Francis had manipulated the situation today
from a stalemate to some sort of partnership. Sure, it
was not necessarily a benevolent one, but still it was a
partnership of sorts, if only because they had agreed to
disagree and were prepared to thrash it out. The
clever, subtle bastard!

Who was the immovable object at this point?

More questions were being asked than answered.
She wasn't sure what was going on. She wasn't sure of
a lot of things any more, certainly not why Francis had

found it so important to make a point of fulfilling a trust. She wasn't even sure whether he had been trying to prove something to her, or to himself.

And just the remembrance of one irrelevant thing sent her over the wobbling edge into hot, wretched tears. It wouldn't have mattered seven, three, even two days ago. But tonight it sheared, the way everything seemed to on this razor-backed rock of a mountain, right through to the bone, and all because this afternoon, in the midst of her dustmote-dancing daydreams, when she had thought back to her very first love, she hadn't even been sure what he had looked like.

CHAPTER FOUR

BY THE end of Monday Kirstie felt as if she had been on the mountain forever, stuck in some kind of weird limbo with Francis where their different pasts were as unreal as a fable and the future had no significance. They were simply co-existing; at best it was a shared purgatory without the cornerstone of a relationship. How he expected them to work out their differences was beyond her—they couldn't even agree on what was black and what was white.

Since time weighed heavily on her hands, she spent most of the day doing odd jobs around the cabin like checking electrical fixtures and crawling through the musty attic rafters to study the condition of the roof. Even though there was always some member of the family popping up for the odd week, without someone in permanent residence it was not unusual to find that something or other had fallen into a state of disrepair.

Francis disappeared to God only knew where in the morning, and took it upon himself in the afternoon to catch their evening supper, which, considering their ample stock of provisions, was only an excuse. Kirstie studied his broad back from the concealment of the nearby trees.

He certainly seemed to be enjoying himself. It awoke a sense of outrage in her. Half clad, as usual, he was stretched out fully along the water's edge, his hold on the fishing-rod negligent to say the least, while has face was turned serenely towards the sun. His closed eyes, the whole power structure of his body, the elegant composition of one hand lying across the flat accordion-ripple of his slim stomach, lips, legs—everything about him was gracefully lax until his fishing-line quivered and grew taut. Then Francis surged into action before Kirstie had even fully realised that he had a bite.

So he was amazingly quick. So he had patience, and the capacity to enjoy everything Kirstie loved about the mountain. So there was beauty and harmony in the fluid performance of his body, and his obvious peace of mind that was such a direct contrast to her own desperate search for it. So what?

Never mind that it was her fault he was here to begin with. Never mind even that the issues that lay between them were far more serious. Kirstie was still flooded by a really righteous pique, because, after all, that was *her* fishing-spot he was trespassing on.

With a sudden upward flex of his arms that sent every muscle down his back undulating, Francis heaved out of the water a sleek silver arc that flapped wildly in a brilliant cascade of sunlit droplets, and he laughed aloud with delight.

'Poacher,' muttered Kirstie, grinding her heel into the spirit of generosity. She turned her back on the enchanting scene and stomped disgustedly away.

Dinner was little more than a glorified mess. Francis insisted on trying to clean and gut the trout himself, and in the process of emulating her efficient technique from the day before he managed to make a thoroughly botched job of it.

Kirstie was standing over him, her arms crossed and eyebrows expressively raised, when he finally sat back on his heels.

'Ah,' said Francis wisely, as with black head bent he contemplated the mangled fillets spread out before him

like a sacrificial offering. 'It looked somewhat easier
when you did it.'

'It helps if you learn how early in your childhood,'
she told him drily. 'I do have about fifteen years'
experience on you.'

He turned an eye up to her. 'Not much good, are
they?'

Surprisingly, the diffidence of that made her unbend
enough to reply with a crooked smile, 'I'm sure you've
had better in New York restaurants, but they'll cook
up all right and, if we're careful about the bones, we
should be able to eat them.'

So Kirstie found herself cooking supper as the sun
went down, and she opened a kitchen window wide to
dissipate the smell of fish while they sat down together
to pick apart their meal. Faced again with the glorious
vitality of Francis's uncomplicated demeanour, she
retreated into her shell like a startled hermit crab and
made a bid to flee soon afterwards. She'd cooked the
supper, hadn't she? Well, he could just get off his
backside and do the dishes.

She nearly made it without any comment from him.
But, as she reached the doorway, his mild voice came
from behind and curled gentle shackles around her
ankles.

'Running away?'

Kirstie's blonde head came up, then she turned to
face him as he looked at her over the steepled fingers.
His kindly emerald regard was a challenge she'd die
before she refused, and her lips tightened briefly before
she replied, 'I have no business with you. All I have to
do is stick this out until after the wedding, if necessary.
You can stay or go as you like. That hasn't changed.'

'But, Kirstie, if I was so hell-bent on Louise, why

would her marriage stop me any more than her engagement did? It still comes down to you and me, right
now, and what might happen when we get back—that
is the real issue,' he told her softly, his gaze almost
sleepy.

'Damn you,' she whispered, shaken, and when she
did reach the sanctuary of her own bedroom it was a
hollow escape.

Cloistered there, she read until midnight and then
pulled on one of her brother's old T-shirts that came
down to her thighs, and went to brush her teeth and
wash her face. The rest of the cabin was in darkness.
Even Francis's room was silent, the door pushed to but
not latched, revealing a crack of space that was pitch-
black. Ridiculously, she gave it a wide berth on her
route back to her own bed where she tried to go to
sleep herself, but only ended up tossing and turning
under the weight of her troubled thoughts.

Would Louise's marriage stop Francis? Kirstie bur-
rowed her forehead into her pillow in frustration. Had
he meant it as a threat, or merely to point out the flaw
in her thinking? But then it would be Neil's duty to
protect Louise, and Louise's responsibility to protect
him. But didn't that mean it was Neil's duty even now,
as Francis said, to fight for their relationship, in spite
of how Louise sought to keep him unaffected?

But—but—but—sputtered in her head like a faulty
engine. At this rate she would never be able to sleep.

Certainly she was wide awake enough to hear the
first stealthy brush of sound from the other side of the
door, but at first she automatically discounted it by
assuming that Francis was making a nocturnal trip to
the bathroom. But when there was no closing of a
door, no evidence of other normal noise, not even the

customary distant gush of the water tap, she perked up and listened curiously.

Swish, swish. That was a strange noise. What could he possibly be doing? There was a loud crash and a rattle that seemed to come just outside her door, then a queer scrabbling, and a slow chill swept down her entire body. Whatever it was, something was horribly wrong.

Nightmarish flashbacks detonated in her head.

He could be capable of anything. . .

She began to tremble violently. After being so very reasonable in his own wretched fashion, oh, why would he do anything now in the middle of the night? Didn't he know it was *dark* out there?

Going to try the reasoning tack? What do we get after that, threats?

He wouldn't. He couldn't, not even he would go that far, she wouldn't believe it of him—God, what was that?

Kirstie bolted upright in bed at the same instant the grey shadow of her door opened silently and, in a culmination of her worst imaginings, Francis glided in. One part of her deep-fried wits managed to take in his supreme caution and how he very carefully latched the door behind him, even as she battled against pure terror to haul in a great lungful of air for an ear-shattering, completely useless scream.

But, when he was quick, he was very, very quick. She didn't have a chance. In one fluid rush he was at her side, and he clamped a hand over her open mouth. It was so large that it covered half her face.

Her whole body jerked with the terrifying shock, but before she had time to give in totally to her unreasoning panic he put his lips to her ear and breathed, 'Be very quiet now.'

His unaffected calm got through to her. She held herself as frozen as a frightened rabbit, and in the stillness of that inaction they both heard the strange, blundering noise again. Now it apeared to be coming from the living-room.

Flooded with a crazy, reeling relief, Kirstie sagged against the warmth of Francis's bare chest and he loosened his grip on her mouth to hold her close. It was a soothing sort of gesture, made absent-mindedly, as all his attention was focused on what was happening on the other side of the door.

'What is it?' she hissed.

'Sh,' he replied, winding his arm around again to touch cautioningly the side of her cheek. 'I don't know. I thought it was you.'

'I thought it was you!' To her amazement she found that she was clinging monkey-like to the solid strength of his waist. She cursed her stupid limbs as they started to shake again with reaction, and he pressed her head down to his shoulder, which smelled deliciously clean.

Then he put his hands to her shoulders to gently ease her away. 'Stay here, all right?'

At the cold touch of metal through the thin T-shirt, she reached out one hand to touch a smooth hard barrel and exclaimed, 'You've got the gun!'

His head bent to hers. 'I don't want to panic you unduly, but what's out there could well be human and unfriendly.'

The sense of their isolation hit her in the gut. 'But there aren't any bullets!'

'They won't know that.' He rose to leave, until she grabbed the hard muscle of his arm.

'You can't go out there! You could be hurt or killed!'

Amazingly, his reaction was to press his lips against her forehead. 'It'll be all right,' he said. 'Just stay put.'

She hadn't had any conscious desire to do otherwise, but when he eased her door open with torturing care, she found herself huddled up behind him and peering anxiously around the broad expanse of his powerful back. He jerked half around and gave her an ungentle push, gritting, 'Get back, you fool!'

And stay here on her own? There wasn't a hope's chance in hell. She swallowed and retorted stoutly, 'I'm not letting you go out there by yourself!'

'Then for God's sake stay behind me!'

He made sure she did by clamping hard fingers around her wrist, one arm twisted, so that for every long, silent step he took she had to scuttle on after. Then he stopped and her nose connected with the spot between his shoulder-blades with a bump. They were at the end of the short hallway, and whatever was bumbling in the dark was still there.

Francis silently pressured her down until she was in a crouch at the corner of the hallway. Then, with a quick squeeze of his fingers, he let go. For a horrible moment she was left alone in the dark, then with a tiny snick light flooded the living-room and at the same time Francis dived sideways across the hall opening in front of her, the gun up and held ready.

He checked immediately and stood straight, looking very odd. At that curiosity overcame her fear, and she put one hand on the floor to lean forward and peer around the corner.

And she looked, eye to eye and on the same level, into an astonished black mask.

The sight was enough to weaken her bent legs so that they slid out from underneath her and she sat with a bump on the cold floor. In reply the fat, whiskered racoon leapt straight into the air, then began to scrabble backwards as fast as it could move.

'Dearie me, our intruder is discombobulated,' Francis commented, with mild hilarity. He leaned back against the wall as his shoulders shook.

'Oh, God!' she gasped. 'How did he get in?'

'I almost hate to mention it. The real question is, how do we get him out?'

'Oh, look at the poor thing! Quick—open all the doors and windows!' The creature cowered between the settee and the wall, its startlingly human paws clapped over its eyes. She hadn't known racoons could get so huge. She scrambled to her feet and darted to the front door to throw it wide, while Francis laid down the gun and began to unlatch the window.

'Be careful,' he warned, looking over his shoulder as she crept around the furniture to get a better look at it. 'You don't want to risk the filthy little beast scratching or biting your legs.'

'How can you call it a filthy little beast?' she said softly, her hands on her bare knees as she bent. 'It's absolutely gorgeous!'

'And probably messing all over the floor in fright,' Francis added, strolling over to the opposite end of the settee. Kirstie glanced at him and realised, for the first time, that he was clad in nothing but his briefs. She gulped and her gaze skittered away as he grasped hold of the furniture and said, 'Get ready.'

He pulled hard at the settee and it screeched woodenly across the bare floor. The racoon exploded out of its corner right towards her. Heavens, she'd never seen anything waddle so fast in her life. Kirstie shouted and waved her arms to shoo it out of the front door, but it didn't get the message.

At the last moment she leapt on to a nearby armchair that teetered dangerously before crashing on to its side, flinging her to the floor. She managed to land on her hands and knees, very much surprised but unhurt, and when she looked around she guffawed to see the bouncing back end of the racoon whisk into the kitchen.

Crying with laughter himself, Francis hurried over to her. 'Are you all right?' he gasped.

'I—I think so. But what about the racoon?' She reached up both hands for his ready grasp and he helped her to her feet.

'I suspect he'll make it out under his own steam now.'

'How?' Hurrying to the kitchen, she found the racoon already gone, the evidence for both his visit and his hasty retreat in the window still wide open from when she'd cooked supper, and the baptism of fish bones scattered all over the counter, stove, floor— even, she found, in the sink. A small pan lay upside-down on the floor, its matching lid in a far-off corner.

'Oh, dear,' she giggled, pointing to the pan as light dawned. 'The crash I heard——'

'—and the rattle,' finished Francis, whose face was still creased with merriment. He wiped his eyes. 'I'm afraid this is all my fault. I put the scraps in the pan to throw out in the morning, and I left the window open to finish airing out the smell of cooked fish.'

'"I don't——"' she stuttered, holding her aching side. '"I don't want to—*panic you unduly*"!'

'Rub it in all you like,' he returned good-naturedly. 'Still, you handled it pretty well.'

'Are you kidding? I was petrified!'

At long last he sobered, the amusement dying slowly out of his expression, and, looking at him, Kirstie was stricken with the thought that the laughter was what had been missing from his face. He sent her a sharp green glance, disturbingly intense, and asked softly,

'Oh, yes? Was that before or after you knew it wasn't me?'

She wasn't prepared for it, and the silken question was like a douche of cold water on her face. She shivered, for her oversized T-shirt had become too thin. Even her skin was too thin, for he had slipped right under it, and she wrapped her arms around herself, a telling, defensive posture.

It was clear from the way he stood, unselfconsciously graceful in only the briefs that covered his male nakedness, that he was braced for the bitter retaliation he obviously expected from her, and the scale of the injustice she had done to him was appallingly evident in the instinctive way he had sought to protect her earlier. Suddenly she knew that he would have done the same for anybody else in their situation.

She wondered if her misjudgement hurt him, and somehow she couldn't bear the possibility of it. She licked her lips and said in a dry, painful whisper, 'But, I——'

Without a change in his intent, dark expression, he stepped up to her and put his hands on to her shoulders. The warmth from his heavy palms anchored her to this place, this unwilling confession. She stared up with huge eyes at his face bent over hers. He whispered back, 'Say it.'

The indecision in her broke. 'Francis,' she said, unaware of how his name came out of her like a cry for reassurance, 'I didn't lock my door!'

How grim the line of his mouth was, how taut. 'So you didn't,' he agreed.

She shook her head from side to side, and he raised one hand to run his fingers through the short hair at the back of her head. The silken strands slipped along the hardened lengths of sinew and bone she felt like iron bands against her skull. He wrapped his other hand around her throat, tilting up her chin, trapping the negative movement of her head.

The very quality of his deliberation was shattering. The room whirled about her so that the only secure point of reference was the rock-like steadiness of his grip. He said with stunning gentleness, 'But perhaps you should have.'

Then his head came down like an avalanche, like a comet. Her heart bucked hard in violent response, but his mouth when he made contact with hers was devastatingly light and hot, sweetly, inexplicably closed to hers, and it was at once an impassioned, feverish caress and a locked door of his own. Dear God, she hadn't a clue whether it was meant to teach her or punish her.

Every one of her senses kicked into hyperdrive. She was vibrantly aware all at once, of not only the very care with which he held her and the utter lack of invasion, but of his scent, and taste, and feel, and, deepest of all, her own growing sensual hunger and disappointment. Not a punishment, but he pushed and pushed her with the long seconds trickling by, and the refusal to either deepen the kiss or pull away, until she gritted under his mouth, both angered and horribly frustrated. 'You don't frighten me!'

Even as she said it, and her mouth opened under his, she knew the statement for what it really was, an invitation.

He froze and, most amazingly of all, the featherlight fingers underneath her chin trembled. Then with exquisite, torturing control, he drew back and they stared at each other, brilliant grey and brilliant green.

'That's all right, then,' he said, so mildly that she felt the urge to hit him, but the white tension had eased from around his mouth. And then, most devastating of all, he released her and turned to walk away.

Kirstie didn't like it.

Francis was up to something. Every inch of his behaviour shouted it. He was still relaxed, even indolent. His eyes laughed more, and when his manner did not tease he was extraordinarily polite. Solicitous. Kirstie finished chewing the nail of her left forefinger and started on the thumb. Charming as well.

In fact, he had been that way ever since their nocturnal visitor on Monday night, and this was a bright Wednesday morning.

She still couldn't believe the utter ease with which he had so sensually, so casually brought her to a silently shrieking peak of physical awareness and then just walked away. She couldn't believe how she had reacted—with fury, with astonishment, with the invitation that she had known he was all too aware of—and how he had refused it and her.

She had run through the entire gamut of emotions. He hadn't wanted to kiss her, really kiss her, to sink into the warm, open crevices of her waiting mouth and devour what she had been prepared to give. That was galling.

Then, after a time, left on that stunned, unfulfilled plateau he had brought her to, she knew differently. She knew, from the unspoken language of his body, with the instinctive feminine awareness of masculine interest, from the way his gaze would linger from time to time on the mobile action of her lips as she spoke, and the stern, banked-down hunger in the depths of those green eyes, that he had wanted to.

She shook herself and jumped out of bed. Yesterday he had awakened her with a smile and breakfast on a tray. He had leaned over the pink bedspread to set the tray across her hips and she had slithered back on her pillows at the first whiff of his fresh warm scent, gaping at the full display of his delectable pectoral muscles only inches away from her mouth.

In any other male she would have liked what she had seen and basked in the attention, but that lazy, patient sexual prowl coming from Francis had her so wound up that if he so much as said boo to her she would be hanging from the ceiling like a cartoon cat.

She had tried, but it was no good any more doing as Francis had suggested on Tuesday morning, which was to take everything one day at a time. He made the urge to gravitate towards him far too easy, and that wasn't possible without concrete answers. Their relationship, already convoluted, had slipped into a place beyond her understanding. She couldn't handle it. She had to get away to think. Making her plans, she crept to the kitchen, heated some water on the stove and measured a teaspoon of instant coffee into a cup, then frowned at it ferociously.

She knew what Francis was up to. She knew, and she also knew why she felt so craven, and why she was going to slip away that morning before he woke up. And she had to make sense of all the riotous confusion that was teeming through her mind, to come to some sort of conclusion, to exorcise the devil of insidious desire he had awakened in her on Monday night.

She had to, because he was waiting, and there would come a time when he wouldn't wait any longer.

She drank her coffee while she dressed, quietly and quickly, then packed some food in one of the backpacks stored in a cupboard below the kichen counters, and eased out of the cabin's front door before seven o'clock.

Then, feeling driven, she set out on her hike in order to find the peace of mind she so desperately needed. She took a path that she had long been familiar with, that skirted around the lake and up to a clear stretch of slope that looked out over a panoramic view.

That isolated place always gave her a feeling of sitting on top of the world. It was silent, windy, far, far away from the noise and congestion of civilisation, and it had never before failed to help her clear her head. She needed that serenity so badly that she put the sight of the dark, gathering clouds out of her mind and continued her climb.

But her concentration was sadly lacking, and as the path skirted along the edge of an overgrown ravine her foot slipped and then her body slipped with her, and with a sharp, startled cry she fell over the edge.

She felt a bruising wrench on her shoulder, a whirling, dizzying sensation of space, and she landed heavily on one hip in a thick, leafy bed of ferns in the bottom of the ravine.

The breath was knocked out of her, so she lay wheezing for a few minutes, waiting to get her strength back before she tried to move. It had been a stupid slip, but she tended to be philosophical about such mishaps, and after her heart had slowed down to normal and she had checked to make sure she hadn't seriously damaged herself she sat up and looked around for her light canvas pack.

She located it at last as it swung back and forth gently, hanging by one strap on the branch of a slender birch sapling, and she scowled at it as she rubbed her sore, scratched shoulder where the pack had rested. Then she squinted at the sky which had shone with such promise just an hour ago, but now looked so sullen, and she could have cried. Nothing had really gone right since she had got out of bed that morning.

As there was nothing else to do, she flexed her fingers and grasped hold of the sapling's smooth, slim trunk to give it a good hard shake. A swallow exploded into flight with a panicked warble and something hit her on the head. Blowing feathers out of her face, she looked around in time to see the bird's nest bounce into the ferns.

'Oh, damn!' she exclaimed in remorse. All she had managed to do so far was to dispossess a bird, and the pack still hung on the branch.

'I'm beginning to think,' said a conversational voice from above, 'that you should be kept on a leash.'

Her heart jolted with surprise and with a supreme effort of will she managed to avoid her head jerking up. It was too much to hope that he would go away if she ignored him, but she was too disconcerted by the way her skin had flushed hot and her limbs begun to shake at the sound of his voice, so she tried anyway and concentrated on narrowing an assessing gaze at the twelve-foot slope in front of her. If one could call it a slope. It was a nearly vertical wall of crumbling soil, rocks and protruding tree-roots, far easier to fall down than to climb up.

'What,' continued the infuriating fellow, 'no glad amazement, no astonished cry of welcome?'

At that Kirstie did glance at him. Francis's green eyes smiled down at her from over the edge, his chin propped in one hand. 'I should have expected you to show up,' she told him flatly. 'All misfortunes come in threes.'

'I must be quite mad,' he said placidly. 'There are far easier maidens to rescue in this world.'

'Did I say I needed rescuing?' she snapped.

'I see you get my point.'

'What happened to my pack? And how did you know I was down here?' Now that he had found her, she was going to have the devil's own time losing him again. She couldn't remember when she had last been so intensely irritated with a man.

'Your pack was well within reach from up here.' He dangled it briefly over the edge to show her. 'And as far as locating you goes, I just happened to be taking a stroll around this side of the lake and followed the sight of this sapling's spasms and the sound of your charming curses. Are you hurt?'

The last had been asked without a change in his calm expression, but the light tone in his voice had gentled so unexpectedly that she felt those stupid, irrational tears prick at the back of her eyes again.

'No,' she replied grudgingly, 'only shaken. Go away.'

He shook his head and a black lock of hair fell into his eyes. 'Not until I see that you're safely out, and soon. In case you hadn't noticed, it's about to rain and, when it does, that ravine is going to fill up with water.'

She tilted back her head and a large raindrop fell on the side of her nose, to trickle tear-like down her cheek. Clenching her teeth, for he was right, she said between them, 'All right, all right. But as soon as I'm out, will you for God's sake leave me alone?'

His expression revealed absolutely nothing. 'If that's what you want,' he agreed equably. 'If you can climb part-way up, I'll lift you the rest of the way out——'

'The thing is, Francis,' she said, her gaze dropping doubtfully to the crumbling wall in front of her, 'I'm not entirely sure it's possible——'

'Of course, if you're not up to a little effort, I can

always go back to the cabin for a length of rope,' he added.

'I'll be right up,' she told him grimly, and started to climb.

The first three feet were easy, but it had begun to rain in earnest. Not only were all the available handholds becoming slick, but the footholds were rapidly dissolving. She managed to scrabble up another half-yard before risking a glance at Francis. He had swung his strong legs over the edge, braced one foot at the base of a young tree that was growing out of the side of the gorge and was leaning over with his hand outstretched.

'Come on,' he encouraged, 'almost there.'

Hot and panting, Kirstie longed to tell him to speak for himself but she didn't have the breath. She peered past a dripping fringe of blonde hair to work out her next handhold. If she went left, then right to the tree Francis was using, she should be able to reach those long, inviting fingers.

The first part of the plan was no problem. She stretched out, arm shaking, tendons straining. Her hand clutched the trunk by Francis's foot; she trusted her weight to her grasp.

'Well done!' he said and reached for her wrist.

But the rain had already done its damage. The tree came loose from its weakened foundation and shuddered forward. Francis rocked off balance. Flat against the side of the gorge, she felt a tiny shower of dislodged dirt and pebbles against her neck as she slipped downwards two feet.

'Look out!' she shouted warningly. He made one more attempt and lunged desperately for her hand. With a creaking and a snapping of roots, the tree broke free. She instinctively ducked her head into her arms as she fell for the second time, crying out as her bruised shoulder connected hard with the ravine floor.

Francis twisted as hard as he could to avoid the impact with her slight-boned body, but he still landed half on top of her. She grunted and he rolled away immediately to come up on his knees and bend over her.

'Dear God,' he said, in a shaken voice quite unlike him. Her eyes flew open, for she had never heard him sound like that before. 'Are you all right?'

'I—I think so,' she whispered, staring up at him.

'Are you sure?' He ran his hands up her legs, probing with care, then checked her arms. Icy shock from both her falls had set in, and the warm, sure touch of his fingers brought a languid, blood-red tide of heat washing over her so that she shivered in convulsive reaction.

Rain had plastered his black hair to his head and ran in rivulets down the side of his neck. He slipped one gentle arm under her shoulders and lifted her against his chest. Turning his vivid green eyes down to hers, he splayed one hand along her side. 'What about your ribs?' he asked.

The ball of his thumb collided with the swell of her breast and, betrayingly, he caught his breath. Electric sexuality crackled through her body as she stared at him, helpless, caught by the wild race of her heart. He had to feel it. It thudded against the palm of his hand. His eyes flared with green fire, and with a tiny clenched shift he cupped her breast.

Her whole body arced in shocked pleasure and as her face tilted upwards he made some small sound at the back of his throat and kissed her, soft as the rain, like the last time, but then his head slanted sideways and he drove between her lips with his hot, seeking tongue, and the last time was banished forever into the past as he hungrily invaded every part of her mouth.

A moan broke from her at the piercing, darting sensation, and he drank the sound away, then unabashedly, voluptuously sucked her tongue into his mouth. She shuddered all over, her one free arm sliding up around his neck, her hand seeking the evocative curve of the nape. It brought him down on top of her, sliding the heavy weight of his torso along hers, an unbearable friction that brought them hip to hip.

His fingers slid over the top of her breast and slowly, tightly raked across the raised nipple he felt through the soaked fabric of her top. Rampant fire shot through her so sharply that her mouth moved, but his was the groan that vibrated through both of their chests. With abrupt urgency, he left her mouth, ran his tongue down the length of her pale, exposed throat and bit at the nipple thrusting so tantalisingly against her T-shirt.

She cried out, twisting underneath him. She was so achingly hot, she felt as if clouds of steam should be rising off her body. His head pulled back up to her face where the skin was tautened over the delicate bones, and as he bent to lick her lips he thrust the bulky, hardened weight between his hips against hers in an ancient communication of desire. It pressed her on to the uneven ground, upon which the rain was pounding, and she lifted her own hips in silent, hungry answer.

And opened her eyes at the same time. And looked at his darkened, heat-flushed face.

Realisation, like a lightning bolt, was fatal in this climate.

Dear God. She looked up and saw Francis Grayson. What was she doing? How could she act like this? A simple touch, a single kiss, and she would have lain back on this fern-filled bed and let him take her. To go from heated passion to being stone-cold sober was as agonising as coming down from a drug. She pulled away from his kiss. His black, wet head reared back. He opened brilliant eyes, but they were blind.

She said stiffly, 'If you're quite through, perhaps we should try that climb again.'

Slowly expression came back to him. She turned her face away from it. 'What happened?' he asked.

'Nothing. Do you mind getting off me? Thank you.'

'What do you mean, nothing happened?' Francis sounded very odd. He sounded too patient, as if he were humouring a recalcitrant child. 'One moment you're with me all the way, and the next it's switched off. What flipped the switch, Kirstie?'

Kirstie pushed herself up on hands and knees, her short hair darkened and plastered flat to her head. 'I'm tired, and this mud feels foul, and all you want to do is sit in a puddle and argue,' she gritted, near to tears, she was so upset with herself. 'Well, argue with yourself. I'm getting out of here.'

The tree she and Francis had dislodged had wedged itself about halfway into the gorge. She scrambled on to it, stood, and swung herself on to the edge at the top. Then, without waiting to see Francis emerge, Kirstie fled—she couldn't kid herself, she knew it—back around the lake towards the cabin.

She got as far as the fishing-hole. At that point she heard Francis behind her. His was a body well trained in short bursts of speed and manoeuvring. Even as her head turned, he scooped her up in both large hands. The impetus of his dash sent them over the edge of the rock.

They hit the lake together. Kirstie screamed in

surprise at the chilly water that closed over her head. All the breath left her body in a choked gasp. She fought to get to the surface as Francis grabbed hold of her again and pulled her head out of the water.

The water was five and a half feet deep at the spot where they had fallen in. Francis could easily stand, whereas Kirstie couldn't touch the bottom. His hands went to her waist and he pulled her against him as she gasped and sputtered.

'Why did you go and do that?' she cried furiously.

His own eyes glittered hot and bright with anger. Water cascaded down his neck and off broad shoulders, and more was falling into his eyes from the sky. He gave her a grim smile. 'Took care of the mud, didn't it?'

Out of sheer temper she splashed his face in retaliation, an action so ridiculous that he laughed, which made her even angrier. 'Let——' kick '——go——' kick '——of me!' In the lake she wasn't able to do much damage, but the last kick against his shins was violent enough to loosen his hold on her waist.

Awkwardly she splashed to the tangled, overgrown shoreline and tried to drag herself out, but the muscle in her left thigh protested against all the abuse she had heaped on it, and cramped. 'Ah!' she cried, doubled up. 'Oh, ouch!'

At once Francis was at her side. As soon as he had climbed out of the water, he reached and picked her up. She was tempted to lash out at him again, but the cramp in her leg was too absorbing. She couldn't even straighten her knee. Evidently he had no desire to rile her further, for when he had reached dry, solid ground he dropped her and strode towards the cabin. She immediately crumpled into a heap, wrapped her arms around her body and shivered.

Francis glanced over his shoulder. When he saw her crouching, bedraggled figure, he walked back to stand in front of her with hands on hips. 'Since you were the one who was so uncomfortable, why aren't you getting up?' he asked suspiciously.

She glared at him through the wet strands in her eyes. 'I would if I c-c-could,' she bit out. 'I've g-got cramp.'

'Heaven give me strength!' He scooped her up again as easily as if she were a ten-pound sack of potatoes and once more strode for the cabin.

Kirstie considered the shape and grace of his collarbone directly in front of her face, bracing herself as well as she could against his chest as she ground her teeth at the painful muscle spasm. The downpour had become a torrent, and the clearing was almost totally dark. So was the cabin as they entered.

'Where's the light switch?' he asked shortly. It was right by his shoulder. She reached out and flicked it on by way of answering.

He crossed the room, set her gently on the settee and started to shove logs from a well-stocked bin into the empty fireplace. A large box of matches was on the mantel. After he had placed logs in a compact, well-designed stack, he lit both ends and soon had a fire going well. The first welcome hint of heat licked across his skin.

He looked at her. Kirstie sat hunched and grimacing over her awkwardly doubled legs. 'I'll go get blankets. Can you strip off those wet clothes by yourself?' he asked.

'I can try,' she muttered, shooting him an annoyed glare.

She managed to unzip her jeans but couldn't get them down her legs when he knelt, dripping, in front of her. 'Look, I'm sorry,' he said when she tried to push his hands away. 'I lost my temper. It was a stupid thing to do. But you've got to get out of those jeans before the heat will do your leg any good. Let me help.'

If looks could kill, God would have had the grace to sizzle him by now. She gave up on her fit of pique, lifted her hips and hissed as he eased the wet denim down both slender white legs. Then she grabbed one of the blankets and wrapped it around her torso.

Francis knelt by her leg and contemplated it with a frown. The muscle spasm was visible to the eye under the velvet skin. 'There's no other way to do this,' he warned. Before she could stop him he had taken firm hold of her thigh and massaged the length of it for several minutes. Kirstie squirmed a frantic protest against the pain, but eventually she was able to uncurl enough to straighten the leg properly.

How strangely comforting, she thought as she watched those long fingers curl around the back of her knee. He was still dripping wet, yet the touch of his hands was warm. As the muscle unclenched, his massaging grew lighter. Seen from that angle, the line of his jaw was beautiful.

What had made him so angry?

'Better now?'

'Yes.'

He looked up and into her open eyes. This time the sexual voltage was so leaping, it seared her to the bone. Her expression filled with dismay; she drew back.

But Francis was already rising smoothly to his feet. 'Fine,' he said, his voice carefully neutral. 'I'll go start you a hot shower. If you stand on under it for a good long time, you won't even be left feeling stiff.'

By the time she remembered to thank him, he was already out of the room.

Forty minutes later, Francis walked out of the bathroom and to his bedroom, a bath-towel slung around his waist, his manner preoccupied. Kirstie's eyes gobbled up the sight of the man, for he was magnificent. She swung out of the living-room chair she had been sitting in and walked into the bathroom.

It was full of steam and Francis's fresh body scent. She could develop quite a reaction to his scent. His sodden clothes were in a pile at one end of the bathtub while hers were still in the sink. The lacy white strap of her bra hung over the side of it. She stuffed it under the shirt while her face burned.

Who would have thought it? Francis Grayson, Wall Street's seventh wonder, kissing skinny little Kirstie Philips from New Jersey. Put like that, the incident in the ravine sounded at best inexplicable. At its very worst it could have been manipulative, coercive.

But she knew better than that. The sensual awareness had been all too apparent in his eyes. Her own face had been naked with it.

She piled the heavy clothes into the laundry basket and threw it outside the door, in a turmoil of disorganised thought. Complications—everything about the man was a complication. Kirstie had no problem with the fact that Francis was supposed to be a very attractive man. She just wasn't supposed to be affected by it.

Today was early afternoon on Wednesday. That meant three more nights alone with him. It was a totally unacceptable computation. She scrapped it and counted up the hours. That, too, sounded astronomically high. What if he tried to kiss her again? What if he tried to seduce her? She'd be putty in his hands, and the worst part was that the fate sounded thoroughly enjoyable.

What if *she* tried to kiss *him*?

With the edge of her sleeve, she polished the bathroom mirror in obsessive circles. Kirstie's imagination on the subject was a bit too vivid. Her body flamed over.

Maybe there was something wrong with her. She stuck out her tongue and looked at it.

'Are you all right?' Francis leaned against the doorpost, eyeing her sceptically.

'Probably not,' she sighed and flinched away from the sight of his hair sprinkled, healthy chest. The least he could do was have the decency to cover himself. She forced herself to stare at him, hard. 'Louise did say one thing that could be taken in your favour. She said you always kept your word. If you were to promise me something, would you stand by it?'

A wary look crept into his eyes. 'If I make a promise, I keep it,' he replied, stressing the first word.

'Can you promise me to keep away from Louise until after the wedding? I mean, not even so much as to give her a phone call?'

'By this I take it you want to go back early and your decision hangs on what I reply to that,' he said, with dry acuteness. A shutter came down over his face. Not by his stance or by so much as a twitch of an eyebrow could she tell what he was thinking. 'No. I won't promise it.'

Did he still want Louise after all? Kirstie had to turn away as a headache began to throb at her temples. She busied herself with straightening the handtowel on its rack. There was utter silence in the doorway until, finally, she turned around to give him a tight, pale smile. 'Get your things ready. We can leave in a half an hour.'

His brows snapped together. She noticed that she had managed to give him a bit of a surprise with that one. After a moment, he said carefully, 'I don't get it.'

'No, I don't suppose you do. Excuse me.' Kirstie brushed past him and went to her bedroom to tidy it and collect the few personal belongings she had brought. He followed.

'Tell me this. Just one thing,' Francis asked sarcastically. 'Does anyone ever understand a single thing you do?'

'Quite frequently,' she muttered.

'Well then, how the hell do they do it?' he snapped.

'How should I know?'

'You're the one who thinks the way you do!'

'Why are you yelling at me? You've got what you wanted all along! You should be over the moon!'

'If I had wanted to just go back, you stupid woman, I would have done so on Sunday!' he roared.

Total silence. They glared at each other. Kirstie was amazed at how Francis looked as if he could throttle her without regret. Instead he pivoted on one heel and stalked away. Her vision blurred. Damn the headache. Damn the man.

She waited deliberately until the dust had settled after his latest bomb. Thinking did no good at all. She was too tired and confused to figure this one out on her own. After a while she went into the living-room and found him sitting in front of the fire, his bare chest gleaming. He stretched his long legs out in front of him and sighed, letting his head fall to the back of the chair, basking in the glow of the fire like a cat.

He looked—peaceful. That black silk fall of hair. She wondered what it would feel like to let the dry strands flow between her fingers. He rolled his head towards her at the sound of her entrance.

'I don't understand you,' she said very quietly.

Just as quietly he replied, 'I know. I'm not so sure I understand it myself.'

She walked to the settee, sat on a very damp patch left earlier by her own wet bottom and with a grimace slid on to the floor. 'What is it you want from me?'

His eyes flashed to her. They looked very light. Twin flames flickered across the lustrous, clear colour. 'It's very simple, idealistic and probably impossible,' he said. 'I want you to accept me for what I am—not what another person told you I am, but what you see right now in front of you.'

The honesty of that was irrefutable, and it hurt like a knife. Her forehead crinkled with the distress it caused, and she whispered, 'Why? Why me, after all I've done to you?'

'Don't you think I've asked myself that?' His lips curved into a little smile, self-mocking, and she saw that he was as pitiless with himself as she was with herself. 'You've kidnapped me, drugged me, threatened me with a gun and disrupted my schedule in one of the most ridiculous, hare-brained schemes I've witnessed in a very long time. I should still be angry with you. I wish I were.'

She closed her eyes. He was giving her too much. I'm sorry, she wanted to say. I'm sorry. But she couldn't.

'The thing is, Kirstie,' Francis was telling her, 'that I can clearly see your concern and desperation in doing what you did. You thought people's lives were being ruined. What you did took courage. You broke the rules of society, but, more importantly, you stayed to face the consequences of what you did, when you didn't have to. And you've continually faced up to your own code of standards even when it meant hurting yourself. I don't agree with what you did, but I can respect it.'

He leaned forward, placed his elbows on his knees. 'Look at me. What do you see?'

'I can't,' she whispered, but she looked at him anyway.

He held her gaze with gentle relentlessness, and then, with the most brutal of all honesties, said, 'You did in the ravine.'

She flinched, and saw how her reaction went right inside him, and even then she couldn't turn away. And then she forced herself to be as brutal as he, as she licked her lips and whispered, 'We both know what happened. When I looked at you in the ravine, I—wanted you. You, Francis. And it was so scary. I—couldn't even blame you, and I wanted to do that too. There's too much between us. I—can't——'

'I know you can't,' he said quietly, shadows flickering across his face. 'And for what it's worth, I blame myself for what happened in the ravine. In itself, it wasn't wrong, but it was at the wrong time, and in the wrong place. And I've never hidden from you who I am or what I've felt, even if it meant shouting at you or making a fool of myself when you've made me angry. Do you see in me the man Louise described to you?'

How honest could she be? How much could this hurt? She breathed hard and broke out in a sweat, but funnily enough it was the disappointment overcoming his own face that hurt most of all. That look loosened her tongue.

'No, I don't,' she said tiredly, and the tension in his whole body eased. 'But I can't decide which is the real

man. Even you admitted there is a ruthless side to you.
It's too much to ask of me. I love her, Francis.'

He closed his eyes, sighed and reached for her fist
that lay cold and clenched on one knee. With gentle
fingers he stroked hers open and warmed them in his
grip. She bent her head and stared, melting into
boneless vulnerability at the generosity of it. 'I know
that too. But truth is only what we see of it. Take the
ugliest woman in the world. If she is loved, she feels
beautiful inside, no matter what her mirror tells her.
And the most beautiful woman in the world can feel
ugly if she fears she is unloved.'

'What are you trying to say to me?' she asked with
difficulty. With each stroke on the inside of her wrist,
it felt as if he were peeling away a layer of cynicism
and disbelief. 'If Louise lied—if—why would she do
such a thing?'

'I don't know,' he said, and she saw another thing.
He too was hurt by what Louise had done. It loosened
another layer. 'I only know that judgement without
mercy is cold, Kirstie.'

Up close his face revealed the imprint of lines, lines
of laughter fanning from those downturned eyes, lines
beside that sensual, firm mouth. There were lines, too,
marking his forehead between the straight black brows
that deepened with anger or determination. It was a
hard face, capable of great softening or ferocious
reaction, but it was not a cruel one.

It was the face she had always seen, from the first,
in the ravine, now. She had recoiled in the ravine, not
from this face, but from the face of the monster painted
inside her head.

She reached out on impulse and curled her small
fingers under his chin. He obeyed the light direction
she applied, looking up swiftly with the openness of

surprise. 'If it were up to me,' she said, 'if it were only me, I would accept without question the person I see.'

His black pupils contracted, his lips parted. He said simply, 'Then we've done all we can here.'

'I want to go home,' she whispered achingly.

He tightened his grip on her hands and nodded. 'So do I, now.'

They tidied the cabin in silence. The rain had slackened off, but it hadn't yet stopped when Francis donned a battered, fishy-smelling anorak and went out to tinker with the helicopter.

Kirstie watched him with a troubled gaze from the shelter of the porch. He had twisted her thinking to a standstill. It was appalling to think of how he had done it with apparent ease, but everything he had said was exactly right according to her way of thinking. Was that because he too operated on a similar wavelength, or was it all a diabolically clever assessment of her personality and weaknesses?

Loyalty to Louise dictated an adherence to the second possibility. Everything she had seen of him supported Francis's honesty. Otherwise his avoidance of returning to New York on Sunday made no sense. And everything he had said was right. Her shoulders sagged. The truth was, she didn't know what to believe, or in whom.

The harsh truth was, she wasn't sure if she wanted to believe in Francis because of what had happened between them while they'd stayed on the mountain. Was she being unfair to Louise's integrity because she found her attraction to Francis impossible to control or deny? Louise *had* lied to Neil, but it was exactly the kind of lie Kirstie would have told to protect someone she loved. And everyone lied at some time or another. Was she too ready to have the seed of doubt sown that

Louise had lied to her too? She wouldn't be able to forgive herself if that were the case. But if Louise had, oh, why?

Her dilemma crystallised into simple clarity, the issues settling on two sides of a coin. One of them was lying. The other wasn't. And she was too involved now; she would be hurt no matter which of them it was. Either way, something of her faith in her people would be ruined, for Francis had managed the very rare. He had climbed inside the circle.

This was the price of the immovable object. Two sides of a coin, flipping in the air, and now it had begun its downward arc. Heads or tails, she lost. And she knew that she didn't want the coin to land, to see what would be staring her in the face.

Francis was in front of her before she realised it, and she recoiled instinctively before she could stop herself. Since she refused to meet his eyes, she failed utterly to see how his facial muscles tightened, how his eyes grew bleak.

'The helicopter is ready,' he told her briefly.

'Fine,' she said, her gaze flicking upwards, then away. He had sounded rather odd. 'Oh, I'd better make sure that the fire in the hearth is cold before we leave. I'll only be five minutes.'

'I'll wait for you out here.'

She poked and prodded until the last lump of ash had crumbled to dust and even she could not find an excuse for delaying any longer. Then, with a heavy sigh, she shut the door on the cabin and went to climb into the pilot's seat.

The blades began to rotate without the slightest hitch. They lifted off the heliport a few moments later. Kirstie shot a look over at the man on her left, but his head was turned away as he watched the cabin fall from sight. She tried to concentrate solely on the flight, but scenes from the last few days kept running through her head.

She was frightened of what she would find at home.

CHAPTER FIVE

THEY were nearing the New Jersey airstrip, the familiar landscape laid out like some marvellously detailed map. Thus far the journey had been conducted in almost total silence. Kirstie closed her mind to any uncertainties, any niggling irrational regrets and concentrated on the landing procedure.

She had just received landing clearance from the control tower when her headphones emitted an electronic screech and her brother Paul's stern voice cut in, 'Kirstie, is that you?'

'Negative, control tower, this is the Red Baron, Snoopy to my friends,' she said and missed the strange look that Francis shot at her. 'Who else would it be? How're Carol and the kids?'

'Wonderful. Normal. No problem, unlike certain relatives of mine,' her brother snapped. 'Do you have any idea what hassles you've caused this week? Sightseeing schedules were disrupted. Flights had to be cancelled——'

'I had a look at the schedules before I took the 'copter, Paul. Try pulling the other leg.'

'In any case,' he continued, bulldoggish to the end, 'you took that 'copter without permission and I want you to report to my office in exactly fifteen minutes.'

'I like this man,' said Francis, holding the spare set of headphones to his left ear. Kirstie speared him with an annoyed sidelong glance. He did not appear to be affected by it. Somewhere on the quiet journey Francis

92

had slipped into what looked to be a remarkably disgusting good mood.

'Do you know what your problem is, Paul?' said Kirstie. 'You have a compulsive personality. You like to play God and know every move everyone makes. I bet you have Carol starch the collar of your pyjama tops. Why don't you try to relax a bit and roll with the punches?'

'Fifteen minutes, Kirstie, and you'd better have a damned good explanation ready or I swear I'll see you grounded for six months.'

'It's your civic duty, pal,' said Francis, grinning widely. 'She's a menace to society.'

'Oh, shut up!' Kirstie snapped, sick of his running commentary.

She had forgotten about her brother, who unfortunately had heard her loud and clear. Paul said ominously, 'On second thoughts, make that ten minutes.'

The heliport by the north hangar was almost directly underneath. Kirstie executed a perfect landing. As the lethal blades slowed to a stop, she drew off the headphones and ran the fingers of both hands through her short blonde hair. Francis twisted in his seat to contemplate her with every sign of fascination

'Hadn't you better get going?' he asked.

'No need.' She tried hard to think straight, but his intent stare was short-circuiting her brain.

'It means you'll be grounded.'

'I will be anyway, since I have no intention of telling him a thing.' The afternoon sun slid along his cheekbones and jaw. It highlighted the laugh-line directly beside his mouth, making the shaven skin look touchable. She turned her head away and muttered to herself, 'Issues, morality, relationships, confrontations. God, I'm sick to death of it.'

That last hadn't been said for Francis's benefit, but he must have extraordinary hearing for, unexpectedly, he laughed. She scowled deeply at the ground outside her window, then arched her back in order to dig into her jeans pocket. Francis's head turned to catch the movement of her hips. She slumped back against her door, tossing a set of keys into his lap. 'Your car's in that garage. Have a nice day.'

His face hardened. After a hesitation he climbed out of the helicopter and slammed the door. Kirstie's mouth drew tight and she breathed hard. Stupid, stupid. Could she really have expected him to do anything else?

Her door was wrenched open.

'What's this?' she cried, falling backwards. Francis caught her by the elbows, swung her to the ground and marched her towards the garage.

'You're coming with me,' he told her, looking insufferably satisfied with himself.

'Oh, no, I'm not!' Kirstie dug in both heels. She found herself grabbed by the waist, slung over his arm fireman-style and carried. This brought her eyes into close focus with his slim buttocks, and watching that particular area of his anatomy move with such swinging grace was an experience so unsettling that she began to sputter.

'You see,' he explained as he stopped to hitch her higher up, 'I've been thinking. You must have known from the start that I wouldn't dream of going to the police with the story of being held up by a five-foot-nothing of a woman. Picture their faces if I were to describe the scenic mountain hideaway where she kept me prisoner for a week without a single demand for ransom. Yes, sir, they'd answer politely, and did you enjoy yourselves?'

Kirstie's head bobbed up and down with every stride. 'You wouldn't,' she guffawed, smirking at the scenario he pithily described. 'Not you. You've got far too much pride for that!'

'Quite. But you didn't honestly think you were going to get away with it so easily, did you? The way I figure it, I owe you a kidnapping.'

'No,' she denied with a shake of her head, still laughing. 'You're too middle-class.'

'Pro-establishment.' With his free hand Francis heaved open the garage doors and strolled towards the BMW. 'Conservative. Boring. Thank you very much.'

Unlocking the door on the left side, he thrust her in first and held on to her wrist as he climbed in afterwards. Then he locked all four doors from the driver's seat and let her go. The car purred to smooth life. They backed out.

Kirstie huddled in her seat and ostentatiously rubbed a wrist that didn't hurt, as she stared at the profile of a man she'd once thought she'd had figured out. As it was, she couldn't count the number of times she had underestimated him. What a nuisance.

'I don't believe this,' she said, with more gloom than incredulity. 'You really mean it.'

'Of course I mean it,' Francis replied, breaking off a little tune he hummed underneath his breath. He speeded up the car. An odd smile tugged the corners of his lips. 'I always mean what I say. Of course, I have considered the possibility that you exude some sort of chemical that affects the rational part of the brain. It's only a working theory, mind you, but I like it.'

Kirstie treated this last dig with frosty silence, slouching down in her seat with arms folded militarily across her chest. She hadn't a clue what Francis wanted from her now, and pride wouldn't allow her to ask him about it. There was something distinctly odd about him, though, a recklessness that had not been in evidence in the man at the beginning of the trip. It was as though he had taken the bit between his teeth and was running hell-for-leather into the wind.

Strangely enough, she wasn't frightened. She could not bring herself to believe in Louise's monster image of Francis enough to believe that he would mean actual harm from what he did. Whatever his reasoning, it was not spite. She would just have to sit back and wait for him to make his point, for at the moment she hadn't any other choice.

Once into New York, Francis had driven more or less automatically to Fifth Avenue. As they passed the Metropolitan Museum of Art in Central Park, he slowed the car to a stop in front of one of the high-rise apartment buildings.

Kirstie piped up for the first time since leaving the airstrip, unashamedly craning her neck to stare around her. 'Excuse me! Did I say middle-class earlier? I should have said upper middle-class, or did your ancestors come over on the Mayflower? You honestly live here?'

He shot her an amused glance. 'I thought you knew everything about me.'

'Yeah, well. Fact seems a little different with experience.'

There was an unreadable look in those wide-set grey eyes of hers. Francis took no chances and grabbed hold of her arm so that she had to scoot across the seat again to get out. He turned to give the keys to a uniformed doorman who had opened his door.

'See that the car is parked, Victor.'

'Certainly, Mr Grayson,' murmured the splendid

fellow, who unbent enough to let his lips twitch upwards in welcome.

As Kirstie trotted past, her forearm in Francis's unbreakable grip, she turned to the doorman and told him, 'Nice to meet you, Victor. I'm being kidnapped.'

For an instant the doorman looked startled, his eyes darting from Francis to his fingers curled around Kirstie's wrist. Then the man snapped his gaze into hyperspace, his expression wooden once more. 'Very good, ma'am.'

She glanced at Francis and saw that he had trouble suppressing a smile. He hurried her through the revolving glass doors before she could do any more damage to the other man's peace of mind.

Kirstie watched as he punched the button to summon a lift, then turned to her. 'I've never known anyone regain their composure quite as fast as you,' he said. As she met his intent green eyes, she sincerely hoped it didn't show how her composure was badly shaken when he slid his hand smoothly over hers, intertwining her fingers in a close clasp. 'Even when you're thrown off balance and reacting to a given situation, some inner ballast seems to take a shift and you're on your feet in no time. Louise doesn't have the trait.'

'Come on, Francis,' she said quietly. 'You and I both know that Louise is no match for you.'

His gaze flickered, but with what, she couldn't tell. 'Another reason for you to take up her battles?' he replied, returning insight for insight. 'Which will be the last battle? When does she start to fight for herself, and stand on her own two feet?'

Kirstie looked away. The lift doors slid open, and they stepped inside.

She kept silent on the ride up, but that was mainly because she had the most bizarre overriding desire to

stop the lift, unbutton Francis's shirt and explore his
bare chest. His fingers still retained a hold of sorts,
sliding against her skin in what seemed to be a preoccupied, unconscious caress. If she moved very nonchal-
antly, her shoulder came into contact with his warm,
solid bicep.

That arm would be quite a mouthful to sink her
teeth into. Tenderly, of course. She bit her lip hard
instead. If there was one thing she found it difficult to
forgive Francis for above all else, it was the way he
had made her so physically aware of him. He had got
his facts twisted around earlier. He was the one who
had flipped her switches, and she had to find a way to
turn them off again for good. Cold, hard sanity alone
had brought her down to earth in the ravine.

She didn't even *want* to want the man. Not him, not
that charming exterior that could make her heart do
delightful, agitated somersaults. Even if—if—Louise
had been mistaken about him, she couldn't afford to
get involved with someone who had such ease in
twisting her thinking and destroying her peace of mind.
There would be no joy in a budding relationship, no
lovemaking, no trust building, no allegiance. Sex with
Francis would be just sex. If she wanted mere physical
exercise she could always double up on aerobics
classes.

They stepped out of the lift into a spacious corridor
with intermittent double doors bordered on either side
by great pottery vases filled with ferns. A woman in
her early forties dressed in a white and black outfit that
looked like something straight out of *Dynasty* came
out of one set of doors just ahead of them, a Pekinese
dog under one arm.

She had a smile for Francis as they passed her, but
all warmth faded from those peacock-blue painted eyes

when they scrutinised Kirstie's undeniably scruffy appearance. 'Maybe she just didn't care for my Nikes, but they were new when I bought them,' whispered Kirstie when they stopped.

Francis laughed as he unlocked the door to his apartment and thrust it open. 'Speak up. Anyone would think you were in church by the way you were acting.'

'I was just wishing I had my camera with me.' Kirstie entered his apartment and looked around with appreciation. The living-room was a large sunken area lined with pale blue couches. The opposite wall was entirely glass, the corner of a metal table and chairs visible through a crack in the curtains. If her sense of direction was right, there would be an excellent view of Central Park from the patio. 'Very trendy. Remind me to be kidnapped more often.'

His mouth twitched wryly, but he didn't comment as he turned away. 'Make yourself at home. I have a few calls to make.'

'You mean I can have the run of the place?'

He looked over his shoulder. Overt delight beamed from Kirstie's face, but the sparkle in her eyes was too sharp for his liking.

He frowned. 'Of course. If you'll excuse me.'

Kirstie wandered through the spacious apartment and grew more and more troubled. In addition to the living-room there were four bedrooms, two with en suite bathrooms, and a study. The kitchen would be a chef's dream, and she'd bet there was a separate dining-room or at the very least a breakfast-nook.

To Kirstie the place was rather like a trip to Disneyland, but Francis hadn't given any of it a second glance. He took it so much for granted that he didn't even show any pride of possession. The whole situation, already tangled past unravelling, had taken another slide away from her. It was beyond all understanding.

After about twenty minutes, Kirstie poked her head around the corner of the kitchen. Francis leaned against the counter and scribbled into a black diary, a phone receiver pinned between his left shoulder and ear. His black hair fell into his eyes and he swiped it back impatiently. He was tousled, casually, attired in another of Paul's outfits from the cabin, but nevertheless looked part of the picture. He darted her a quick glance and held up a finger.

'. . .Right. That's fine. Thanks a lot, Mrs Callihan. I probably won't see you tomorrow as I'll be working late, but I'll leave a grocery list on the counter.'

Kirstie said as he hung up, 'An IBM computer in the study, an Austrian crystal chess-set on an ivory and mahogany board, televisions and videos in each of the bedrooms—did you know that you have over fifty of those handmade suits hanging in your closet? And that's some jacuzzi in your bathroom. Can I try it before I leave?'

Francis stared at her very hard, eyes narrowed. 'That's some inventory check you've conducted. Get to the point.'

Her brow wrinkled as she lifted herself to a sitting position on the counter opposite him and idly swung her legs. 'You see, Francis, the more I look around, the more things don't add up.'

'You know about my position at Amalgamated Trust.' He folded his arms and tilted his head back. 'Do you have any idea what that job entails?'

'Simplistically, you make money make money.' She hunched her shoulders. 'I knew you were successful, but after looking at this, my estimate is that you have to be on a seven-figure income.'

'My kind of expertise is well paid for. As it happens, the apartment is rented by the corporation, but the furnishings are mine and in any case I could afford to pay the rent if I had to. Why doesn't that add up?'

'It's not in the possessions, but what they imply. We've got a bit of money in the family, but a lot of it is sunk into the aircraft and radar equipment. We're lucky; the business is solvent, we have good contracts for regional shipping, and the tourist sideline that I handle brings in a tidy amount of change. I suppose it's rather despotic to say we're well capable of providing for our own. But we're nowhere near your league.'

Francis considered her as if he'd never seen her before. 'I didn't realise you were so materialistic.'

'I'm not!' she said impatiently. 'You're not getting the point. Look at yourself objectively. You move among the cream of New York. A lot of your associates are probably old money. You could and probably have dated world-class models, débutantes, women novelists, even English aristocracy. Like all of us, Louise has had her chance at a good education and the choice of whether or not to help out in the business, but she teaches high-school chemistry, for God's sake. Francis, why her after all these years?'

'I'm no sexual athlete, Kirstie,' he told her quietly. 'A seventy- to eighty-hour working week is not conducive to the kind of life you're building up in your mind.'

She made a quick gesture with one hand. 'You wouldn't have to be. Louise is lovely, but, if you don't mind my saying so, you're one hell of a catch. All I'm getting at is that you must have your pick of dozens of attractive women if you're that way inclined. Are you in love with my sister? It can't be simple sexuality. I just don't understand, that's all.'

'Yet you were the one who shed the most honest

light on the situation, however flippantly you meant it,' he replied. Her gaze was locked with his. Those green eyes of his were most beautiful with expression. 'Perhaps when I looked her up I did want to make a trip down memory lane. Life tasted different with a little suspense. We didn't know what the future would hold for us, but we were eager to find out. Tedium played no part in our dreams. I wanted to remember what spring was like again.'

'But spring comes every year. It shouldn't be just a memory,' she said, and for the first time since he had known her there was uncomplicated compassion in Kirstie's expression. He saw it and smiled. She came down off her counter perch, and without thinking reached for both of his hands. 'Francis, could you have made some mistake? Could you have somehow pressurised Louise without realising it?'

She was begging for some kind of explanation to ease her nagging doubt; she knew it and didn't care. His eyes darkened as he looked down at her upturned face. He cupped her cheek in what looked like sorrow, and gave her own words back to her. 'I can't, Kirstie. It's too much to ask of me.'

She bent her head and turned away.

Francis stirred and became brisk. 'Are you hungry? I'm starving.'

It was a deliberate move on his part, another extension of the olive-branch, and with an effort she took the distraction he offered. 'I could eat. What have you got?'

'Probably nothing edible after five days away.' He picked up a Yellow Pages directory that was by the phone. 'Why don't I get a pizza delivered?'

'Fine, anything.'

She was staring at the floor. She didn't see his

sympathetic glance. 'You can raid my wine-rack if you like.' With one finger on the page, he picked up the receiver.

Kirstie shook off her worries, opened the refrigerator door and stuck her head inside. 'Got any beer?'

They ate the pizza straight from the box outside on the balcony, washing it down with Miller Lite. By some strange miracle they managed to preserve the companionable atmosphere begun so briefly in Vermont.

Francis had changed into some of his own clothes, casual steel-grey trousers and a pale pink shirt. Kirstie decided that pink suited him. His black hair looked more glossy, his eyes even more vivid. After all that wood-chopping, his face had acquired a brown tan which also suited him.

'By the way,' he told her, propping his feet in an empty chair, 'you're kidnapped until Louise gets here at nine.'

She was silent for a moment, brooding. So this was the way it would be handled, then? A myriad emotions swirled inside like dustdevils raised by a storm, every one of them aching. There would be no winner in the confrontation, but all she said was, 'At least I can get a ride home with her.'

The night sky was purple while below them the street lights glowed. The concrete floor of the balcony still retained much of the daytime heat, contrasting with gusts of cooling breeze.

'You have a most atypical attitude towards all this. I don't know why it should surprise me,' he said abruptly.

Kirstie saw no reason why she shouldn't be honest with him. 'What other way is there to be? I haven't so much as a wooden nickel in these jeans, so unless you provided either transportation or let me use your phone I didn't have a great deal of choice, did I?'

'Didn't you mind being kidnapped and forced into this against your will?'

'Didn't I deserve it?' Their gazes clashed. She asked, deliberately indifferent, 'Are you still sore about yours?'

'Oh, no,' he said comfortably. 'I'm still miffed about that middle-class crack, though.'

'You're not,' she said, and laughed. She couldn't help herself.

'I am.' He sent her a level look and the skin along Kirstie's upper arms tingled. 'You don't know me at all, do you?'

Her smile faded. Unbidden, an electric image of the gully burned her retina. 'Should I?' she whispered.

Through the open glass door, they both heard the buzz of the intercom from across the living-room. Francis rose to his feet leisurely. 'That will be Louise downstairs.'

He went inside, and Kirstie's mind threw her into rollercoaster loops. What was it she didn't understand about Francis? Which man did she believe in? Of course he was charming, but the devil himself was said to be a gentleman. Yes, indeed he knew how to fit himself to one's mood, which could be as comforting as a well-loved slipper. But wasn't that in itself a manipulation?

It was a rocky ride she was on. If she went any faster or was thrown on any more loops, she felt as if she might crash off the beaten track, and there was a hell of a drop to the ground.

It didn't bear thinking about. She was tearing herself into pieces. Kirstie slammed the cardboard lid back on the left-over pizza savagely.

Francis had waited by the front door. She twisted in her seat when she heard a light, impatient knock. What had he said to her sister in order to make her come? She saw Francis hesitate and look towards the balcony. He opened the door. And Kirstie saw Louise step inside and throw her arms around his neck.

This was the loop in the ride.

The blood left Kirstie's face. She couldn't breathe. She rose very carefully. Put one foot in front of another. Touched the door-handle to see if it was real. She looked down at her hand. Force the fingers apart. Let go, Kirstie.

'—and your secretary just kept putting me off,' her sister was saying. Abundant golden hair tumbled down her back, unlike Kirstie's untidy wisps. Louise raised a hand to Francis's face—he hadn't moved since opening the door. 'Why didn't you call if you couldn't make our date on Friday? I've been half out of my mind.'

And Kirstie went too fast on that ride.

'Louise,' said Francis. He put both hands to her upper arms and gently pushed her away.

And Kirstie went over the edge, and fell.

'Hello, Louise,' she said quietly. Francis looked at her. With a startled gasp, the other woman whirled. 'I cancelled the date for you after we talked on Thursday night. I see I don't know what is going on after all.'

'Oh, God,' said Louise, too high and much too fast. 'What are you doing here? You're supposed to be on a business trip! Do you two know each other? How do you two know each other? Kirstie, you must believe me, it isn't what you think. Damn you, I told you to stay away!'

'I see,' she said. She took a seat at one end of the couch. Francis had never seen Kirstie's face so blank, her eyes such a bottomless black.

'I think you don't,' said Francis.

Louise was as slight as Kirstie, with velvet blue eyes and a heart-shaped face. She looked nowhere near her age at the best of times. Now she seemed no more than a wretched child as she twisted her fingers through the strap of her bag. Though there was nine years' difference between them, Kirstie felt ancient at the sight of her.

'Did you honestly think I could stay away, after your superbly heartwrenching cry for help?' she asked, her voice a harsh scrape of sound. 'Why, Louise? I've never known you to lie to me before.'

'I don't know. I didn't mean to, but you were so close to finding out. It's just—I'm thirty-five years old. Seeing him made me feel as if I were twenty again. I never wanted to hurt anyone, or cause so much trouble. It's just that I'm so confused,' Louise whispered. Her blue eyes clung to Kirstie and begged.

Kirstie looked down at the knees of her jeans. She smoothed slow fingers over the material. She thought of last Friday, and Francis's anger. She thought of the helicopter and the cabin, and fresh-water trout. She thought of Louise staring at herself in a mirror, being frightened of the wrinkles she saw beginning to line her face. A new pain hit her hard in the chest.

At first it was difficult to speak. She asked, 'Are you going to marry Neil on Saturday?'

For a long moment Louise's gaze darted back and forth between her younger sister and Francis. All his attention was on Kirstie and he was silent. 'I—I don't——' Louise said.

'Are you, or aren't you, Louise?' Francis asked. His face was hard, a closed book, giving nothing to either of them.

Louise searched his face, but he looked almost

bored, and her lips tightened until she was an ugly sight. 'Yes,' she said, and the single uttered word was cold.

Patience fought the pain and disillusionment inside Kirstie and won. She stood, walked over to Louise and put one arm around her. 'Then we should be finished with this business. It's gone too far. Let's go home.'

Louise bowed her head and nodded. Kirstie walked with her to the door, then turned back to look at Francis. From a statuesque stillness, he had come to life with the most strange expression. How odd it must be for him to say goodbye a second time to his past.

'Kirstie——' He took two rapid steps forward, held out one hand.

'I'm so sorry. For everything,' she told him. The pain rose in her eyes, now grey as a rain-filled summer day.

'It doesn't have to be like this, you know.'

'I know of no other way it can be.' He had been the victim in all ways, in this messy cauldron of mixed emotions. She could give him one more thing; she had that much left in her. She smiled just a little, saw the sight of it hit him like a blow and said, 'Goodbye, Francis. Be happy.'

Kirstie's trip with her sister down the lift to the lobby of the apartment building was made in utter silence.

Victor the doorman was kept rather occupied as they passed him, for he held the leashes of three excitable afghan hounds who had run around him enough times to effectively truss him like a turkey. As Kirstie stared at the scene without really taking it in, Louise led the way to her parked car.

Although the older woman still looked shell-shocked, the colour was beginning to flood back to her

cheeks in two red spots and her eyes regained their
bright diamond glitter. When Kirstie had climbed into
the passenger seat, it was to confront her sister lounging comfortably, one slim arm over the top of the
steering-wheel, the blue eyes vivid.

After a moment, Louise said, softly, 'Whoever
would have thought it?'

Kirstie closed her eyes. God, if it was one thing she
wasn't in the mood for, it was a post mortem. 'What
do you mean?' she asked tiredly, although she knew
full well.

'You,' said Louise. Her fingernails tapped a gentle
rhythm against the wheel. 'Braving the lion in his den,
so to speak. You must have broken all sorts of records
in returning from your trip. Have you even been home
yet?'

She raised one hand to run it through her short-
cropped hair, making the wispy ends even more wild.
Then she turned her head, met Louise's curious stare
and said flatly, 'I never went. There was no business
trip. I took the helicopter, took Francis and flew to
Vermont for the weekend.'

That shook Louise's new-found composure. The
fingernail tapping stopped, her pretty mouth dropped
and she all but shrieked, '*You what?*'

'You heard what I said.' Kirstie turned away to look
out of her window. She saw nothing of the wide city
street but thought again of the hot, bright sunshine
reflected off the still lake waters. She made a wry,
sarcastic gesture. 'Not that he wanted to go, of course.
I forced him. I was going to keep him away from you
until your wedding on Saturday, but he—convinced
me it was better to get hold of you so that we could all
talk about it face to face.'

'You—forced—Francis?' Parrot-like, her sister

repeated the words as if they were a foreign language. Then she started to laugh. 'You're joking! Aren't you?'

'Not,' said Kirstie, heavy with remorse, 'quite.'

'But how? I mean—Francis, of all people—forgive me, darling, but you couldn't exactly have twisted his arm!'

'No,' she agreed, her grey eyes empty. 'I used Dad's old gun. Oh, there weren't any bullets in it, but he didn't know that, and at first he didn't know me from Eve.'

'But how could you?' Louise demanded incredulously. 'How dared you?'

The shock in her sister's voice made her throw her hand out in a sudden, sharp movement. 'Oh, I don't know!' she exclaimed. 'I admit it was a lunatic thing to do, but——' Kirstie stabbed her sister with a fierce, painful glance. She whispered fiercely, 'Maybe you just thought to cover your tracks, but you don't know how convincing you can be!'

'Oh, Kirstie,' Louise murmured, her cornflower eyes filling with easy tears. Her right hand fluttered out to touch Kirstie's shoulder. 'And you did all that for me. I—I don't know what to say.'

'Don't say anything.' She slid down in her seat, put her elbow to her open window and covered her eyes in an effort to hold on to her control. It was her responsibility. It always had been. She was the one who had to live with the fact that what she had done to Francis was unforgivable. 'Just don't ever do that to me again.'

Left with nothing to say, Louise moved at last to start the car and take them home. The gaudy, multi-coloured lights advertising off-licences, fast-food restaurants, late-night grocers, hotels, all flashed past them with what seemed like brilliant speed. It was a totally different world from the log cabin, and it was the real one.

Kirstie stared at it all passing by until she was shaken out of her brooding by the light sound of Louise's sudden inexplicable laugh. 'Fancy that,' said Louise softly, as her small foot pressed down on the accelerator as they reached the freeway. The wind whipped her sister's long silken strands into a luscious, honeyed cloud. 'You and Francis spending a whole, secluded weekend up at the cabin. It sounds—it sounds so very intimate!'

'Don't make me laugh!' Kirstie snarled, as if lashed by a whip.

But Louise must have misunderstood and thought she meant it light-heartedly, for at that her sister laughed again.

CHAPTER SIX

SUMMER percolated into July, with no significant let-up from the heat. Shirts stuck to sweaty backs, the Coke machine in the Philips Aviation offices broke down from over-use and tempers were undeniably short.

One Friday morning, Kirstie perched cross-legged on a wooden crate in the small hold of the cargo plane and took inventory of the stock being brought aboard. She was dressed in a khaki flying suit made of the lightest possible fabric, and still she was baking. Her grandfather Whit was grumbling and roaring at the ground crew; the irascible shouts echoed up the hatch and seemed magnified in the confined space where she crouched.

She'd volunteered for the inventory job, for, though it was physically rather uncomfortable, it was purely mechanical and left her free to huddle in a corner and let her mind wander where it would.

It had been four smouldering weeks since the Bomb. Kirstie always referred to Louise's wedding fiasco that way. It had her shaking her head just to remember the day. The invited guests had arrived, the minister had been dressing in the choir room, Neil had been to one side talking with his best man, and Louise had refused to budge. Point-blank.

Their eldest brother Paul had tried to reason with her. The minister had come. Neil had come. So had Grandma and Whit. They had all talked. The brides-maids had cajoled. The minister had left and called off the wedding in a formal announcement to the congregation, while, tucked away in a corner, Kirstie had watched the commencing drama with horror and her other brother Christian had laughed.

Something of Kirstie's perspective had changed since the time spent in Vermont with Francis, and she had begun to see a disturbing pattern developing in Louise's behaviour.

After the ruckus had died down, after the guests had left and the wedding decorations had been dismantled and carted away, Kirstie had gone back to the house she had shared with Louise with a cold feeling in her heart, and waited.

The scene she had expected was not long in coming. . .

Louise came in later that evening, her eyes swollen with crying, her pretty face wearing an expression of haggard distress. When she saw Kirstie curled up at one end of the battered comfortable sofa, she made a move as if she would throw herself into her younger sister's arms, but something in Kirstie's expression stopped her.

Kirstie watched Louise pause and drag in a deep, shuddering breath. 'Well,' said Louise heavily, 'that's it. It's done.'

'Yes,' replied Kirstie quietly.

The china-blue eyes flickered and one of Louise's shapely, graceful hands fluttered up to press against her wrinkled forehead. 'How could I have waited so long without realising?' Louise murmured. 'How could I have fooled myself into believing that marriage with Neil was the right thing to do?'

'I don't know,' said Kirstie, and she was rewarded with a sharp glance.

Louise glided over to an armchair and flung herself

into it, burying her face in her hands. 'It's just that it seemed so expected. Everyone believed we would marry! His family did, Grandma, Paul, you. It was so easy to go along with it.'

'Until the last moment, when everyone was hurt.' Kirstie didn't feel cold or condemning, nor did she sound it. She was merely detached, and she couldn't give Louise the sympathy she was so obviously angling for.

Louise lifted her head, her blue eyes flooding with easy tears. 'Until today,' she corrected, 'when I just couldn't go through with it. No matter how painful it was, no matter how unbearable the look in Neil's eyes, I had to call it off, for his sake as much as for mine. The marriage wouldn't have worked and he would have been hurt as well. It was best to end it before we both put years into a marriage that was destined to fail. What if we'd had children? What would have happened to them?'

'Why are you explaining all this to me?' Kirstie asked, her hands clenched on the cushion she was holding to her stomach, her mouth tight. She already knew what her sister's answer would be. She'd heard it before.

Louise said softly, gently, 'Because you don't understand. You never would have left it until the last minute. You would have seen. You're stronger than I am.'

Now, perspiring in the metal hold of the little plane and immersed in her gritty work, Kirstie realised that something inside her had been waiting for Louise to back out of the wedding, ever since that final confrontation in Francis's apartment. All the signs had been evident. Louise had thought she had wanted Neil, then was presented with a bigger, more glittering toy, so she'd thrown away the one she had had.

It was not, she knew, that her sister was malicious or wicked. It was just that Louise was supremely selfish. She did whatever she wanted to do, and she justified it to whichever person she was talking to in their own language. She enjoyed acting out the required emotions. Everyone thought they knew her well, Paul, Grandma, Neil—even she had.

Christian knew better. Kirstie had always wondered at Louise's coolness towards him, and now she knew why. Her tall, charmingly irresponsible brother saw Louise for what she really was and was unaffected, even amused by her. If it was one thing Louise did not have, it was a sense of humour. She was as incapable of laughing at herself as she was of passing a mirror without looking into it.

Kirstie's newer, more complete understanding of her sister changed her definition of Francis's kidnap from being a terrible misunderstanding to a ridiculous farce, except she couldn't bring herself to laugh at it. Louise had thought she was being so clever in manipulating her, until Kirstie had gone off at the deep end and had done something totally uncalculated. Louise was not a creative thinker. There was no way she could have foreseen it.

And Francis—an appalled sound bubbled out of Kirstie—Francis had been totally in the dark. Every incredulous look she could remember, every sign of incomprehension was now, to her, hideously appropriate. How carefully he had worked at bringing her around to a reasonable point of view! What a lunatic he must think her!

No, Kirstie couldn't laugh about it. Depression settled in the pit of her stomach at just thinking about that whole catastrophic weekend. If she were ever to come face to face again with Francis Grayson, she would pull up the carpet and crawl right underneath. Not that it would ever happen. She had no doubt that she was enough reason to make him avoid the whole state of New Jersey.

She wondered, cynically, how long it would take Louise to get in touch with him again. Then she told herself, as she already had, so many times, that it was none of her business. Of course she didn't care.

Why would she?

Footsteps stomped up to the open hatch, and her grandfather stuck his grizzled head inside. 'Hey! That's the last. Didn't you hear me?'

The testy exclamation made Kirstie jump. She shook herself out of her reverie and stared at him. 'Sorry, no. I was thinking of something else.'

'Well, I hope you got the tally right,' he said. 'We ain't unstacking and repacking in this heat just because you were daydreaming.'

'No, it's all right,' Kirstie said, checking her figures. 'I got them all down. I just wasn't listening to your shouting.'

'That's the trouble,' mumbled her grandfather, screwing his face into a frown. She stared, amused. Heavens, he enjoyed a good grumble. 'If people listened to me more, I wouldn't have to shout, would I? Well, what are you waiting for, Christmas? Climb on out of there and get this crate off the tarmac. You should have left a half an hour ago.'

'Yes, Grandpa,' said Kirstie meekly, a smile trembling at the corners of her lips.

His faded blue eyes twinkled at her, making a lie of his behaviour. Then he ducked back out and howled at his ground crew, 'Go on, get out of here! Go get some lunch, and give me some peace for an hour.'

The plane was already fuelled, checked and set to go. Kirstie was given priority as she was late, and within ten minutes she taxied down the runway, experiencing as she always did an uplift of spirits as the plane rose in the air.

An undeniable streak of mischief made her radio in to control, 'I estimate arrival in Memphis at 0200 hours——'

The radio squawked in consternation, and Paul overrode their air traffic controller to snap, 'Negative, that's an inaccurate flight plan, Kirstie. your destination in Cincinnati, repeat, Cincinnati, not Memphis——'

She smiled and put her pilot's sunglasses on. 'Just making sure you're on your toes. I'll be back around seven this evening. Who's staying to see me in?'

There was a pause. 'I am,' said her brother, then, with disgust, 'so don't be late.'

Because the weather was in her favour, Kirstie made up for lost time and landed in Cincinnati on schedule. She had a late lunch of coffee and sandwiches while the plane was being unloaded, then headed back to New Jersey with the setting sun behind her, humming tunelessly and switching radio frequencies to amuse herself.

Normally the four full-time pilots, of whom Christian was one, drew straws as to who worked late on Friday, but she didn't mind making the Cincinnati run this week since she hadn't much planned for the evening. She hoped that Louise would be going out so that she could relax in peace, perhaps mess about in the kitchen fixing supper and watch some television.

Kirstie's social circle was wide enough that she had

no shortage of dates when she wanted it, but it lacked the hectic quality of Louise's lifestyle. Kirstie was just as happy soaking in a bath and enjoying her own company, whereas Louise was out almost every night of the week and resented having to stay in the odd evening to mark papers.

Coming in the last leg of her journey, she contacted control, received clearance which by this time was just a formality as everyone else should be grounded, and she lined up for her descent.

'Look out the window and wave, Paul,' she called in, and dipped her wings back and forth when the control tower came into sight.

Paul's long-suffering attitude was apparent, even over the radio. 'Why me, Kirstie? I know your professional reputation. You're on time, you're efficient, polite, no hassle. It's never anyone else but me.'

Kirstie tilted the plane to one side again. 'You're just so cute when you're teased. I wouldn't do it if I didn't love you.'

'Try landing the plane right side up like a good girl, and behave yourself,' he said, drily resigned, against a background of laughter. 'You're on the loudspeaker and we've got company.'

She was too startled to do anything else but comply, and she executed a perfect landing with the careless flourish of a professional, afterwards taxiing the plane to the appropriate hangar. She wondered who was at the tower after business hours. Carol sometimes came to pick up her husband, but Paul wouldn't have called family 'company'.

Outside the plane, the waiting ground crew ran to put wheel blocks into place while Kirstie unstrapped herself and began to shut down the engine. Paul came over the air again. 'How long before you can come to the tower, Kirstie?'

She drew her brows together and replied, 'I wasn't planning on doing the paperwork tonight. The inventory was checked, and the Cincinnati firm's happy.'

'That's all right, leave it till Monday. You've got somebody waiting here to see you.'

She had 'company', and her puzzled frown deepened. 'Roger, be there in five minutes.'

Who could it be? She wasn't expecting anyone, had no date for tonight, and it was apparently nobody Paul knew. She wondered as she strolled towards the tower and main offices, pushing her sunglasses up her nose. It was still hot, and she was parched with thirst. She hoped the Coke machine had been fixed that afternoon; she'd threatened Paul with a strike if it hadn't, and she dug for some change as she walked down the hall towards it.

The contrary machine took her money and did nothing. She slammed her frustrated fist into it, and it spat out three cans with a pathetic whine. Then it spat out all its money. She watched with amusement as the quarters spilled on to the floor.

'Hey, Paul!' she shouted. 'The drinks machine is really broken this time, but never mind. I just hit jackpot.'

She bent the tab of her drink back and raised her laughing gaze as someone strolled around the end of the hall. But it wasn't her brother Paul coming to investigate; it was Francis Grayson, nonchalant and bigger than life, his hands tucked in the trouser pockets of his suit.

Shock froze her where she stood, and in the few seconds it took him to reach her she noticed a host of irrelevant things: how the burnished newness of his tan had faded, how vivid his lazy emerald eyes were, how the fitting of his suit to that athletically formed body was superb. She also had time to think of how she was attired, and curse her inevitable luck at the small battered Nikes, the serviceable flying suit, how her short hair was thrust off her heat-flushed face.

She was glad she had her dark pilot's glasses to hide behind as he stopped in front of her and smiled slowly. 'Hello.'

'Hello yourself.' For lack of anything better to do, she tilted her head back and drank, all too aware of his gaze on her long, exposed throat. She then told him, 'You wouldn't exactly have been my first guess as to who was waiting for me.'

'No?' His green eyes blinked secretively. 'Who would have been your first guess?'

She ignored that and bent to scoop up the extra Coke and the quarters. 'What can I do for you?' How have you been? Have you forgiven, and forgotten?

'You can go out with me tonight.' She dropped one of the cans, and his long-fingered hand beat hers to picking it up. 'I need to talk to you.'

Ah. Comprehension dawned at his second sentence, and she was glad she had kept what was visible of her face under tight rein. She said, 'Louise.'

He didn't respond to that; he merely asked, 'Will you come?'

She turned away in silence and strode for the lit control-room, with her hands full of money, and two cans of Coke tucked in her arm. Francis matched her shorter stride, and just before the doorway he put one hand on her arm so that she had to stop.

'Please,' he said.

She had asked herself many questions during that short silence, and one of them was whether she really would or not, so she already knew what she was going to say. 'All right. I owe you that.'

Inside the control-room was her curious elder brother, but she wasn't about to indulge any of his obvious hints. She just deposited the quarters and extra can on the table beside Paul, while Francis handed him the third can and said goodnight. She could feel Paul's eyes boring into her back as they walked out of the room. At the doorway she glanced back in time to see him bend the tab back of the Coke he was holding, and he yelled as the disturbed brown liquid sprayed all over his face and desk.

Laughing again, she followed Francis out to the street exit, looking at Philips Aviation through the eyes of a stranger. In comparison to any international airport, this set-up was like a toy, but it was an impressive-looking toy. Half the buildings were new, the other half pristine. The general air was one of precision and competence. That would appeal to Francis, she knew.

She dragged to a halt by the car park, the sight of the BMW evoking an odd, bittersweet regret inside her. Francis was one stride behind, noticing her stop, and he pivoted on one heel back to her, an easy, thoughtless movement that seemed to her half completed. In her mind she finished it for him, took one step forward and threw her arms around his neck in an uncomplicated gladness.

Disturbed, she looked at her own battered car. 'What did you have in mind?' she asked, when he seemed content just to stare at her, immersed in his private thoughts. 'I—I'm afraid I can't invite you back to my place, since Louise lives with me, and I don't know whether she's going out tonight or not. Shall I meet you some place? I'll go home and change into something more presentable.'

'Don't bother. You look fine.' Then, as she emitted an incredulous laugh, he swept his leisurely glance down her as if assessing her anew. He reached out and ran a light finger down the neckline of the collar, straightening it so delicately that she could not feel his touch, yet she shivered as if a strong wind had blown through her. 'No, I mean it. You look comfortable. I like it. In fact, if I could use the Gents here I'll do the changing, into a pair of jeans I keep in my boot. Do you mind waiting?'

'Of course not,' she said, still staring at him.

'Be right back.' He sprinted to his car and retrieved the jeans and a pair of tennis shoes every bit as battered as her own. He waved them to her and disappeared into the building, while she was left flooded with the images of his apartment and alien wealth, yet with the memory of their companionability.

And the memory of their too brief spontaneous combustion. They had both moved as one towards the drinking from each other's lips. She remembered, remembered everything. Her fingers rose to press against her lips, dragging hard against the sensitive swell of flesh. She must be quite mad. Was she here to help him get Louise back? Why did he need to speak to her alone? What was there to say that hadn't been said already?

Another indelible image burnt like a brand. Francis, cupping her cold, clenched hand and stroking it with warm tenderness. So much hadn't been said.

'Are you all right?'

She whirled, fully caught in the intimacy of her musing, her head rearing back with as much shock as if he had caught her naked. Francis's eyes were too knowing, too sympathetic, as if he read her thoughts and shared them, but that was she being fanciful. 'I'm fine,' she replied, the sound harsh from frozen throat muscles. 'Where are we going?'

'Get in my car, I'll drive.'

But she shook her head, and the attention he gave even that slight movement of hers made her wonder if she did so with undue violence. 'I can't leave mine, it'll be locked in for the weekend.'

'Then I'll follow you home,' he replied, and his eyes lit with inexplicable amusement. 'You can park in your street without getting caught, can't you?'

She tilted her head shortly, an unwilling acknowledgement at how reasonable that sounded. 'All right, why not?'

'Fine, lead the way.'

They were heading towards New York and Friday evening traffic was travelling against them, so they made good time. Kirstie tried not to think of how incongruous her humble little Datsun seemed with the gleaming, immaculate BMW purring close behind.

As with the airstrip, she saw the town where she lived through the eyes of a stranger as they drove through. Upper Montclair, New Jersey, was rolling with gentle hills and wide, paved avenues. It was a lovely shady place in the daytime. Now, the darkened treetops rustled as the wind swooshed through them, seeking open spaces. The large colonial-style houses they passed as she slowed preparatory to turning into her street were set well back, with long driveways ribboning through spacious front gardens.

With the property boom in recent years, the prices of houses now were such that Kirstie couldn't afford to move here, but her parents' house had been paid for on their deaths by their insurance policy.

She could imagine how Francis would find the interior, long since redecorated with a feminine touch. She slowed her car to a crawl, wound down her window and motioned for Francis to pull to one side. After waiting to see that he did, she speeded up until, about a hundred yards down the street and with a keen sense of the ridiculous, she switched off her engine and let her car coast silently into her driveway.

When it had rolled to a stop, she moved fast, locking her doors and grabbing her bag as she eased the door on to its latch, with a quick glance towards the lit front window. Since they always left that light on, she couldn't tell if Louise was home or not, but she wasn't taking any chances and raced swiftly back to the street, her blonde head thrown back to watch for Francis.

Car headlights came on from fifty yards away, the twin beams blinding her. She raised a hand to her face, and the ghostly BMW purred to an elegant stop in front of her. The passenger door was pushed open from within.

Francis said smoothly, 'Climb in, and the world's our oyster.'

Kirstie tumbled in, laughing, and as she slammed her door shut the car shot away. Francis rolled the sun-roof back and the windows down, letting in the wild evening wind. The BMW ate up the neighbourhood streets until they reached the interstate highway and accumulated speed with an effortlessness that made their earlier pace seem as though they'd been sitting still.

Francis threw her a sidelong glance. It was as though he was a totally different person from the precise businessman at the airstrip, with his wind-ruffled hair and faded jeans, and his white shirt open at the neck to leave his strong throat free of restriction. She sensed the latent maleness in the length and breadth of his thighs, sewn into the larger, stronger bone and sinew, a psychic sniff that was like an exotic perfume. It was heady and perturbing, a dangerously addictive drug that wrapped itself around her jangling nerves.

'What were you laughing at when you climbed in?' he asked.

Kirstie shrugged, looking out of her own window to give herself the illusion of space away from this disturbing man. 'At how silly the whole charade was, I guess. It reminded me of when I was a teenager. My bedroom window on the second floor overlooks the garage roof and I used to sneak out of it, across the roof, and down the large oak tree on the opposite side. It seemed a clever thing to do—until I got caught.'

She heard the silent exhalation of his laugh and slanted a look back at him in time to see him sober. He said, 'Louise told me how your parents died in a car accident. I was sorry to hear it; I'd never met them, but I liked what I knew about them.'

She lifted a shoulder in helpless reaction against an old ache. 'They were pretty neat people. They had a good deal of common sense and a whole lot of love. It was a combination that managed to keep them pretty sane through the raising of four kids.' Then, almost in the same breath, 'Francis, where are we going?'

'Does it matter?' he countered. The smile had crept back around the edges of his mobile, fascinating mouth.

The dull ache, a baffling grief, still hurt her chest. She ignored it and replied, wryly, 'We don't have to go this far out to talk about Louise.'

'But there's no reason why we can't enjoy ourselves while we do it, is there?' He lifted one hand from the wheel and spread it out fingers up, a graceful offering made with a turn of his wrist. 'The night is made for magic. The Manhattan skyline, Greenwich Village jazz, Little Italy and Chinatown restaurants, Harlem funk. It's all ahead. It can be ours for the experience.'

He made a whole night of possibilities appear in what he said, in that little gesture. He brought to her a cruel fantasy of simple pleasure, and she wanted it.

Kirstie didn't mind confusion. Not really, not as long as it was confined to items, events and other people. She became distressed, however, when the confusion was inside her, and Francis prompted a screaming riot of conflicting emotions and desires. It had taken several weeks, but she had just got her life back to some semblance of normality, haunted only by memory and self-denial, when he had to reappear and sent her back on to that rollercoaster ride.

Of course the best way to alleviate the confusion was to avoid him. After tonight that was exactly what she intended to do, and she would stop thinking about him as well. He wanted to talk to her about Louise, so she would listen and sympathise as best she could with whatever it was that troubled him. And, when the evening was over, so too would her phantom guilt be eradicated. They could go their inevitable separate ways.

Having thus mapped out the immediate future to her complete satisfaction, Kirstie slid down in her seat, swamped in misery at what she felt sure would bring her peace of mind.

CHAPTER SEVEN

FRANCIS asked Kirstie what kind of evening she preferred and, thinking it would be better than the intimacy of more quiet settings, she opted for a nightclub. Once she was in the packed Soho club, however, Kirstie began to have second thoughts.

Francis went ahead to forge a path through the crowd, the fingers of one hand locked firmly around hers. Kirstie scuttled along with her nose buried in Francis's shirt-sheathed back.

Someone jostled her, and she fell into him with a bump. Francis twisted around and put a protective arm around her shoulders, drawing her against his side. The slightly raised calluses on his palm rasped against the tiny sensitive hairs on her upper arms, and her resulting shiver was violent.

His voice rumbled in her ear and vibrated through her ribcage. 'What do you want to drink?'

'Scotch,' said Kirstie, her heart knocking like a faulty engine. She looked away, unable to meet that lazy, jewel-like gleam bending down towards her. 'Make it a double, please.'

For some reason that made him laugh. 'There never are any half-measures with you, are there?' She turned back to stare at him, but he was already walking to the bar.

Francis leaned against the bar-top and ordered Kirstie's Scotch, along with a tonic and lemon for him, as he was driving. Kirstie looked around at the nightclub with interest, for it had been Francis's choice. The place had more character than elegance, and the crowd was rowdy and expansive. Most of the men wore jeans, though several women were attired in clinging dresses and high heels. Nevertheless, Kirstie did not feel out of place in her casual clothes.

It was not exactly the sort of place that she would have thought Francis even knew about, let alone where he would go out of choice. If she had thought about it at all, she would have imagined him surrounded by civilised expense, where all the waiters and waitresses talked in hushed whispers and champagne was priced at hundreds of dollars per bottle.

With a pang she finished painting the picture in her mind. Louise's voluptuous beauty, clothed in designer fashion, Cartier jewellery and handmade Italian shoes would fit in perfectly.

'Penny for them,' murmured a voice in her ear. She jumped as Francis pressed a glass full of amber liquid into her hands. He was too close, the music too loud; she would have to put her mouth right up to the lean line of his jaw in order to make herself heard at all. Instead she just smiled and shook her head.

He smiled back. 'Come on, I've found a space at the bar.' So, feeling like an obedient dummy, she followed him to the empty bar stool where they placed their drinks. Francis turned back to her, sliding his hands down her arms to her elbows to make the small jump to her waist as he helped her hop on to the high perch.

She swivelled to the bar counter and nursed her drink, huddling over it while Francis lounged by her side. He did not seem in any hurry to delve into conversation, though, and watched the people around him with alert interest. Her eyes followed the curve of black hair at the nape of his strong neck and met the avid, hungry gaze of a woman from the opposite side of the bar, who had been appreciating the same view. Instant antagonism flared with a growl inside Kirstie. She glanced away abruptly, shocked.

'What do you think, do you like the place?' asked Francis beside her.

She kept her face averted. 'It's got character.'

'Kirstie,' he said. She turned her head. Their gazes, mere inches apart, connected with a shock. His patient emerald eyes sparkled with the reflections of the brightly coloured directed lights. 'I thought we might be able to enjoy ourselves a little, but you haven't relaxed since we walked through the door.'

'I'm sorry,' she muttered, shivering inside as his gaze shifted down to her lips. 'I've got a lot on my mind.'

He accepted that without prying and told her, 'If you want to go, we can go.'

He sounded indifferent, as if it didn't matter, and it woke the perverse side of Kirstie's normally easygoing nature. She had acted the fool, sneaked her car into her own driveway, travelled for more than an hour to get here, only to turn right around and leave? 'No,' she said, taking a swallow of her drink. It burned in her stomach, spreading a reckless warmth. 'That's all right, we can stay.'

'Well, for a moment I was worried, but judging by your enthusiasm you must be having the time of your life,' he said, and the sarcasm was so accurately thrust that it surprised her into staring at him.

Heavens, what was wrong with her? She hadn't said or done anything right since he'd appeared at the airstrip. Kirstie stuttered with contrition, 'I am sorry— I didn't mean—what I meant to say was——'

Then Francis surprised her even more as he burst out laughing. Amusement lit his whole face, and she had just enough time to realise that he had been teasing her when he set down his own drink and took hold of her arm. 'Come on, you ridiculous creature,' said Francis, dragging her off the stool 'There's no talking reason with you at the moment, so we may as well dance.'

He led her on to the packed dance-floor and pulled her against his chest. There, indeed, all reason deserted her as he wrapped both arms firmly around her and held her tight, despite all her attempts to put some distance between them.

Frantic heat coursed through her body. Kirstie turned her head away, wild to look anywhere but at where his shirt-buttons parted to reveal hair-sprinkled skin. He bent his head and put his lips to the shell of her ear, murmuring wickedly, 'What's the matter, Kirstie? You're as stiff as a board.'

'This isn't the right music for slow dancing,' she hissed.

'Ah, but there's no room for anything else. Be a sport. Put your arms around my neck and pretend you like this.'

Like this? *Like* this? Her composure was in smoking ruins, her thinking a débâcle. This was a disaster; this was madness. This was unbearable pleasure, with his thighs rubbing gracefully against hers, his torso a perfect haven. All her senses were vibrantly aware of the length and breadth of his body, his scent and warmth. Her fingers slid up to his shoulders and tightened. She meant to push him away, to set herself free, but, when he buried his face into her hypersensitive neck and inhaled slow and deep, all the strength trickled out of her arms.

His hands moved down the curve of her spine, moulding her body against the taut, muscle-ridged length of his. She could feel every hollow and bulge through her thin flying suit, even the rough, sturdy barrier of jeans at his hips. Her breasts were pressed hard against his chest, the double barriers of their clothing no protection from the sensation of the soft twin mounds of flesh thudding with her heartbeat, thudding into him. With a slow, deep sigh he brought his head down and laid it gently against hers.

She caught her breath in a trembling moan that cut through the chest-thudding beat of the music, and, as always, lost her battle to react against Francis.

His armament was fantastic. He had the thrust of the intellect, the ability to manoeuvre conversations, a sense of humour, and, most importantly of all, he laid all those weapons down and succumbed to this simplistic, silent quest for animal comfort. It made him vulnerable, and that was his most secret weapon of all, for his vulnerability crumbled her common sense and veiled her mind from the thought of future consequence.

She was shaking like a leaf and flailed mentally for some kind of secure point to hold on to. 'Stop it,' she groaned.

He lifted his head and his arms tightened, gathering her even closer. She looked up and his eyes, green and narrowed, were quizzically puzzled. 'Why?' he asked quietly. 'Am I hurting you? Are you hurting me?'

Her head was too heavy and fell on to his waiting shoulder. 'No—yes. Because—because——'

'Because you're afraid you might want it?' he asked gently.

She had no reason to give him the answer; self-protection alone should have stopped her. She held very still and after long seconds whispered, 'Yes.'

Was that a tremble in his limbs. Did she imagine his low groan? Blocking the flashing lights, he bent his cheek to her head. When she might have lifted her face, he cupped the back of her neck with both heavy hands. His heart was racing out of control, thudding through his whole body like a midnight train, and she was the one who pressed hard against him, felt the butterfly flutter of his ridged stomach muscles, the damp heat making his shirt cling to him, the stunning, mind-destroying evidence of the hardened pressure pounding low between his hips that thrust its aggressive male urgency into the soft pit of her abdomen. Her answering rhythmic ache was an emptiness that was a physical pain.

This had never happened to her before, not even with that first, distant love-affair. This elemental compulsion was totally outside her experience; she had no controls, no barriers to erect and pull her back, for she had never needed them. Her breath came fast as inside she careened towards a breaking-point. So very close; she was almost there; they could both sense it. Her eyes closed, her head turned, her mouth seeking the erratic pulse-point at his open neck, and his hands guided her.

Then a rambunctious laughing couple bumped into them and the moment splintered. Both Kirstie and Francis staggered. The other woman struggled to get her balance but couldn't avoid falling into Kirstie, who was knocked out of Francis's arms.

''Scuse me!'' burbled the tipsy blonde as she hung on to Kirstie. For a moment it was impossible to tell who supported whom, then, with a strained smile, she straightened away from the other woman, who lurched back to her companion.

A brief interruption, but more than enough. She had time for realisation, for a brief sense of furious regret, and finally a return to sanity. She had time for a

desperate clutch at her composure until Francis laid his
hands on her shoulders and turned her around to face
him. Then, as his gaze rested on her face for a long
moment and his expression changed, she had time to
ask the first thing that popped into her head.

'When did Louise get in touch with you?'

He went still and hesitated, a direct contrast to the
dancing people and loud music. A succession of
thoughts ran at the back of his gaze, too fast to
interpret. 'A couple of weeks ago,' he said. 'The first
time. Then on Tuesday this week.'

Kirstie was too tired suddenly to hide her cynicism.
'And when did you see her?'

'I haven't.' Anger, then, from him.

Her grey eyes flashed—with derision, disbelief? She
didn't know. 'Not even now that she's free?'

His grip on her tightened, and his gaze snapped into
sharp query. 'What do you mean, now that she's free?'

'Didn't she tell you? Oh, I am surprised,' she murmured, faltering at his evident incomprehension.

His jaw jutted out with furious, bitten-back aggression. 'My secretary took both calls,' he enunciated,
practically shaking her with every word. 'I didn't talk
to Louise! What did you think of me, that I would see
her behind her new husband's back?'

'I didn't mean that!' she cried, feeling as if her
collarbones were being crushed. 'I would have thought
she'd have told you: she didn't marry Neil! She called
the wedding off, Francis!'

That went in past the suddenly blank face. His eyes
flickered, but his hold on her never eased. She wondered if he even knew what he was doing. 'That's why
she's still living with you?'

'Yes!'

'Well, well,' he said with sudden vivid interest. 'This is a pretty kettle of fish.'

Kirstie couldn't look at him. She had to get away, and she twisted from underneath his hands with a force that hurt. 'I'm going to the ladies' room. Excuse me.'

Francis let her go. He didn't try to stop her.

Kirstie threaded her way through the crowd on the floor, her head whirling with the aftermath of shock and confusion. She stepped carefully around a couple and into someone. As she turned to apologise to the man, she caught a strong whiff of alcohol and her nostrils pinched in involuntary distaste. 'Excuse me,' she said, her voice distant.

'Hey, honey,' said the stranger, his eyes running down her figure, 'this must be my lucky night. You're not leaving the dance-floor so soon? The evening's just started!'

He caught hold of her wrists and leaned forward. He was thicker in build than Francis or either of her brothers, with blunt features and great ham-like hands. His suggestive touch made her skin crawl. She avoided his eyes and tried to pull away, replying lightly, 'I hope you enjoy it.'

'I intend to,' he leered.

'But not with me,' she said, and yanked her hands down as hard as she could.

'Wait!' he reached for her again, but his reactions were slowed by drink. Kirstie skipped through a gap, took the stairs off the dance-floor two at a time and fled to the ladies' room.

Surprisingly, the room was empty. Kirstie splashed cold water on her face and leaned for a long moment over the sink, her head in her hands.

The whole thing was starting again, and it was so typical. The arguments, the misunderstandings. The carnival ride. He hadn't known Louise was still single. That was why he'd wanted to talk to her. He had seduced her into thinking they really could enjoy themselves on the most simplistic level, without undercurrents, and he had held her with such insidious sensuality when he hadn't known Louise was still single.

She had trapped herself so easily. It was so effortless to sink into his presence, to bury herself in mindless sensation, to forget about consequences and concentrate on nothing but the moment. To pull away from it was like suffering from withdrawal symptoms. She felt cold, starving. She remembered wanting his heat. Kirstie fought herself with single-minded intensity, forcing down the ache, then turned and violently yanked a paper towel from the metal holder. She wiped her face and scrubbed her neck until the skin was dry, then reluctantly went to face whatever was waiting for her in the outside world.

The short hall leading back to the main area of the nightclub as crowded. Kirstie negotiated it with her head down, deep in thought. A large figure moved to block her way, but she didn't notice until she bumped into the man. He grabbed her arms.

Up snapped her head. This was like a bad recurring dream. She narrowed eyes gone suddenly hard at the drunken man from the dance-floor. 'I don't think you know what you're getting into.'

'Hey, sugar.' The man grinned and bent over her, either not hearing or ignoring her frosty reception. 'You ran away too fast the last time. Lemme buy you a drink.'

'No, thank you.' She tried to prise his sausage fingers off her, but they tightened.

'Oh, baby, don't be that way. It's Friday night. Time

to party! Maybe you and me can go some place quieter. Would you like that?'

His heavy body bore her backwards, into the wall. Disgust snapped Kirstie's patience. She hissed into the man's face, 'Take your hands off me. While you're at it, take your offensive breath and your boorish manners some place else. For the last time, I'm not interested!'

The man opened his bloodshot eyes wide. 'Whoa, look out, it's a haughty bitch! What's the matter, princess, a working man not good enough for you?'

'You have no social skills whatsoever,' Kirstie informed the man. With a violent shove, she managed to break his hold. He staggered back, clipped a phone booth with one shoulder and sat down on the floor hard. Sighing with relief, she entered the main section and began the long walk back to the bar. As soon as she found Francis, she was going to tell him she wanted to go home. She'd had just about all she could take.

But her relief was short-lived. The drunk seized her wrist and jerked her around to face him. 'Nobody does that to me, you hear that, princess? Nobody!'

His grip was bruising. The last thing she needed tonight was a meat-tank with a tiny mind in an ugly mood. Irritably Kirstie tried to tug away. 'For God's sake, fellow! Back down, you're way out of line!'

A nearby man who had been watching this exchange suggested, 'The lady doesn't appear to like your attentions. Why don't you take a hike?'

Her drunk didn't take too kindly to the interruption and snarled an unprintable suggestion. The two men bristled at each other like a pair of bulldogs. The people surrounding the trio began to move away. Kirstie noticed and sighed.

'Look, there's no need——' she began.

'Butt out,' said the drunk. A good forty pounds lighter, her would-be rescuer flicked an uncertain glance around, obviously having second thoughts about his role in the scene.

Furious, she jabbed a stiff finger into the drunk's chest. 'You started this. You're pushing it. You got a bee in your bonnet, so take it outside, bucko! People here are trying to have a good time. They don't need this.'

'I said butt out.' He seemed to barely touch her shoulder, but the push knocked her flat. Kirstie bumped into a table as she went down, sending drinks flying. The surrounding crowd bubbled and hissed like a pressure cooker.

Francis appeared out of nowhere. She didn't even see him move. One moment she was sitting on the floor, the next he stood straddling her legs in direct confrontation with the beefy agitator.

Kirstie wanted to lean her head against the back of his knee. Francis would handle the situation. Everything would be all right. She couldn't see the glitter of his green, polished glass eyes. The drunk flexed his right hand and smiled.

'Are you OK?' Francis asked quietly over his shoulder.

'Yes, thanks.'

'That's all right, then,' he said, and hit the drunk square on the jaw. The man pivoted in one complete circle and sat down hard on another table, knocking a bucket of melting ice on to the lap of a woman who jumped to her feet with a shriek. Her escort surged upright also, took hold of the drunk and pushed him on to the floor.

Kirstie scrambled to her feet behind Francis and

shouted, 'Why'd you do that? Are you crazy? You're crazy!'

The drunk fought to his feet and said happily, 'You asked for it, you son of a bitch.'

He swung. Francis ducked. Kirstie didn't. The punch was meant for the jaw of a taller man and would have broken hers had it connected. Instead, the great clenched fist skimmed the top of her head and knocked her off balance. Kirstie fell once more and decided that the floor was the best place for her.

The drunk teetered from the force of his thrown punch. Francis straightened and clapped both hands on the back of his shoulders. The man immediately began to box at empty air. 'Kirstie?' Francis said, still sounding as calm as ever.

'Yes?' she said from underneath the table.

'Get out the front door and wait for me.' He swung his body around at the hips and tossed the drunk over the nearby railing, on to the dance-floor. The noisy crowd surged back and forth. Men rushed into the fray, and women ran away from it. The last glimpse Kirstie had of Francis was of him stepping neatly back from another pair of fighting men while a chair sailed through the air.

Kirstie ducked her head and crawled. She went as quickly as she could to the nearest wall, stood up and inched towards the exit. The whole nightclub had gone mad, and fighting was breaking out in every corner. A man went down in front of her, and she jumped over him as he struggled to his knees. Another fell into her, and she was slammed into the wall so hard it knocked the breath out of her. Coughing painfully, she wriggled out from behind him and weaved her way on. Just when she thought she would never get to the front doors, she was swept up in a massive surge of people and could do nothing but fight to keep her footing.

The crowd carried her to a side exit that opened into an alleyway, some of them still fighting. Panic welled up inside as she wondered if she would ever get out of the fray. When would the police arrive? Would Francis make it outside? What if he didn't? As a rather small female she went relatively unnoticed, but he was large, male and fair game for anyone wanting to pick a quarrel.

He could be hurt seriously. People could die in this sort of fracas.

There was a lot more open space in the street, and she was nearly there. The distant wail of sirens provided fresh fuel to the writhing mass. Someone crashed into her back and she tumbled out of the alley with more haste than she intended to, caught herself up and turned anxiously towards the front entrance.

Miracle of miracles, she recognised the back of the only man fighting to get back inside the nightclub, and she stopped at the edge of the crowd and shouted over the pandemonium, 'Francis!'

His head lifted, the black hair ruffled now and falling over the brow of a very grim expression. His eyes flashed dangerously as they skimmed over the people. She shouted again, saw him catch sight of her, and intense relief flooded his face. He abandoned the door, pushed out of the crowd and raced to her.

The sirens were much louder and closer now. Francis took her face in both hands and urgently examined it. 'You're hurt?'

'No?' Puzzlement made her answer sound like a question as she stared up at him.

He closed his eyes briefly, then said, 'Come on.'

He led her at a run down the street and around the

corner. They didn't stop until they had reached the car which was parked two blocks away. Normally a dash of that distance wouldn't have winded her, but her chest was still sore from when she'd had the wind knocked out of her. Kirstie bent over and propped her hands on her knees, panting, while Francis dug out his keys and quickly unlocked the passenger door.

'Climb in,' he said tersely, waiting until her door was locked. He raced around the other side, let himself in, and locked his as well. He swung around in his seat to look at her with a frown. 'Are you sure you're all right?'

She gasped, 'I had the wind knocked out of me! It still hurts. I'm OK, though.'

'Come here, let me look at your face.' He turned on the interior light and gently tilted her face up towards it. Long gentle fingers probed one cheekbone. As she winced, he asked, 'That tender?'

'Yes. I must have hit it when I fell into the wall.' Her eyes focused on him. His black hair gleamed like jet, and harsh lines scored marks beside his mouth. His green eyes were quietly alert, and where someone had hit him by the mouth there was a shadow that was darker than the short growth of beard. 'What about you?'

He brushed the enquiry aside impatiently, exploring the bump past the edge of her hairline. 'Don't worry about me.'

She hadn't foreseen the end of her fuse, but Francis had just lit it. The inside of her head exploded. 'Fine, that's great to know for the next time, isn't it? I'll know better than to worry, won't I? It's rather nice to know what to expect, if you're going to throw punches like there's no tomorrow! Whatever possessed you?'

He considered her steadily, the evidence of strain

and the remnant of fear still dilating her grey eyes, the shock and the upset she was bitterly trying to control. He slid his hands to her neck and began to massage where the tendons stood against the thin delicate skin, and he said with quiet simplicity, 'The man pushed you down. It made me mad. I lost my temper, when the first sight of trouble in places like that can make them flare like tinderboxes. I didn't think fast enough to the consequences. No excuses.'

Her eyes wavered and fell at the unexpected scope of his honesty, and with a sigh the tension flowed out of her. 'That man was hellbent on destruction. There was simply no reasoning with him, so I don't really think you could have stopped it from happening,' she muttered. 'I shouldn't have yelled at you. It's just that—you really scared me, Francis.'

'*I* scared *you*?' With a groan he hauled her against his chest, holding her fiercely and shaking his head over her, for all the world as if she were some new-found precious chick and he the clucking hen. '*You* frightened the daylights out of me! When I got outside and found you weren't there, I was frantic to get back inside! How did you get past me?'

'I didn't,' she told him, her voice muffled against his chest. She abandoned pretence and common sense and buried her face in the vital comfort. 'I got pushed out of a side exit and came up behind you.'

A heavy sigh shook his chest. With one hand he reached for the interior light and flicked it off. When Kirstie glanced up, Francis was studying the street for signs of disturbance, scenting the air like a hound. At her movement he brought one hand up and stroked her hair absently. 'We should go,' he said finally. 'It isn't safe here. I'll take you back to my place.'

She stirred at that suggestion, disturbed at the

thought of his elegant empty apartment. 'No,' she replied slowly, bringing her wristwatch up. 'It's late. You'd better take me home instead.'

His green eyes came back to her speculatively. 'You need an ice-pack for your sore cheek.'

She couldn't look at him. 'I can fix one at home.'

'We still haven't really talked.'

'I know.' She pushed herself upright and his arms fell away. 'But I—I'm too tired to face it tonight.'

There was a little silence that went on too long. She turned, stared down the length of the darkened pavement.

'I'll call you next week.'

'Fine. That's fine.'

He tried to see her expression, wouldn't leave it alone. 'You will come?'

Kirstie made a gesture which felt so awkward that she tucked her arm close to her side right afterwards. 'I don't know why.'

'Don't you?' he asked oddly, and she sent a furtive sideways glance at his impassive face. With an unsmiling shrug, he reached forward and started the engine.

The trip back to Montclair was silent. Kirstie rode with her head back on the rest, lethargic after the unexpected stresses of the evening. Francis was preoccupied, concentrating on the road with a frown. He seemed so thoroughly self-contained as to be unapproachable, and she wondered if she should say something and, if so, what it would be.

There were so many things she wanted to ask, but it wasn't the time or the place, and she certainly didn't have the right. When they turned on to her street and pulled up by the house, she looked at him across the widening gulf between them and knew it was insurmountable.

'I'll call you,' he said. She gave a little nod, while wondering if he would. And at the last he reached forward and touched her sore cheek with a gentleness that brought a wet sheen to her eyes.

She knew she couldn't reply without making an utter fool of herself, so instead she just turned and got out of the car. All her thoughts were behind her with the man in the silver BMW that purred down the street into the night. That was why she never saw the twitch of a curtain at the lit front window, or the shadow of the woman that moved away.

CHAPTER EIGHT

THERE was no sign of Louise when Kirstie let herself quietly into the house. She breathed a silent word of thanks, negotiated her way around the squeaky third stair from the top of the staircase and locked herself in the bathroom.

A quick study of her reflection assured her that, though her cheek was a bit swollen and red, it wouldn't necessarily bruise. She stripped off all her clothing, turned on the shower and stepped into it with a long-drawn-out sigh.

The hot, steamy water jetted down on her slim body, washing away all the accumulated aches and tension. After working overtime for most of the evening, her numb mind refused to work any more, and like an automaton she soaped all over, rinsed, and dried off.

With the towel wrapped around her sarong-fashion, she slipped out of the bathroom and into her bedroom, sparing a quick glance at Louise's closed door. It looked as if at least some measure of luck was with her. She could afford to relax and not worry about what tomorrow would bring. Kirstie drew an oversized nightshirt over her damp body and, without even bothering to comb her tangled hair, she fell into bed and slept like the dead.

The morning came far too early. Kirstie surfaced out of a murky dream to the sound of someone knocking on her bedroom door. She rolled over, stretched and groaned at the protest of stiff muscles. Her cheek where it pressed into her pillow was tender. So too was the top of her head when she ran her fingers through her hair.

'What do you want?' she croaked.

'Good morning!' called Louise cheerily. 'I'm cooking breakfast and wanted to know how many eggs you could eat!'

'None!' The thought of food made her stomach distinctly unhappy, and she huddled into a ball under her blankets. 'I don't want any breakfast. Thanks anyway.'

'Oh, come on, Kirstie! I've already got the bacon cooking, and coffee made. You'll wake up after you've had a cup. I'll go get you one.'

For whatever reason, Louise was not about to let her pretend that Saturday hadn't come and, lacking the strength for any more shouted arguments, Kirstie gave in. She cleared her throat and called out resignedly, 'No, don't bother. I'll be downstairs in a few minutes.'

'Good,' said Louise with satisfaction. 'See you then.'

Having committed herself, Kirstie swung her feet to the floor and sat on the edge of the bed, yawning. She glanced at her clock and found to her horror that it was just eight-thirty in the morning.

Then, as she shook off the last remnants of sleep, she sat still under the first wave of cold, clear thought. What in the world was Louise doing up at eight-thirty? Her sister was a habitual late riser on the weekends, and for that reason alone rarely cooked breakfast as it was usually lunchtime before she was hungry. Kirstie went to wash her face and then pulled on jeans and a sweatshirt, to the tune of alarm bells ringing caution in her head.

Downstairs in the kitchen, Kirstie found Louise humming under her breath as she buttered a piece of toast. The older woman looked enchanting wrapped in a pale pink dressing-gown with a ruffled collar, her golden curls tumbling from a carelessly used rubber band. 'Coffee coming up in a moment,' she said, as Kirstie eased into a chair at the table. Louise turned and briskly set the toast in front of her, along with an empty mug into which she poured the steaming aromatic brew.

'Thanks,' muttered Kirstie with a sarcasm she was sure her sister wouldn't catch. She pushed away her toast and took her mug to sip at it delicately.

Louise brought to the table a plate full of bacon and scrambled eggs and took the seat opposite her. 'It's a beautiful morning,' she said. 'Have you seen it?'

Kirstie shook her head. 'No, I was too busy sleeping.'

'Ah,' nodded her sister. She took a bite of toast and watched Kirstie sharply. 'Late night, was it?'

Kirstie almost smiled. So that was the reason for the breakfast and expansive mood. Louise was curious about where she was last night and wanted to pump her for information. 'Something like that,' she agreed.

'Did you go out all by yourself?'

The question seemed innocuous enough, but Kirstie was too wise to fall into that trap, and leaving her car in the driveway was a clear indicator otherwise. She ignored the question and asked one of her own. 'Were you in last night? I didn't think to check.'

There was a silence. 'Yes,' replied her sister.

Kirstie affected remorse. 'If we'd known, you could have come out with us. I went into New York with a friend of a friend. We didn't do anything exciting, just ended up at the cinema.'

Louise stabbed another piece of egg without looking up. 'Do I know the man?'

'I'm not sure you do,' replied Kirstie quietly.

Louise's lips thinned into a humourless smile, her blue eyes cold. 'Gallivanting around New York with a mystery man in tow,' she said lightly. 'If you're not careful, you could make me jealous.'

So she suspected, but didn't know for sure. Having Louise as an enemy was a startling and sobering thought. Kirstie raised her eyebrows and replied, just as lightly, 'I stand warned.'

By Wednesday Francis still hadn't called, which was no more than she had expected. Kirstie kept very busy, very reasonable, and struggled with her temper which was unaccountably volatile. The tourist business was running strong throughout the summer months. She patiently ferried a rich Texan and his beautiful, spoiled wife around the New York sights and at the end of the day walked into the central offices of Philips Aviation with a fifty-dollar tip tucked in the back pocket of her jeans.

'How did it go?' asked Paul when she reported back at his office.

'Well enough, I suppose,' sighed Kirstie, as she rubbed at her tired eyes.

Her older brother looked nothing like his blond siblings, favouring their father's side of the family with straight brown hair, pleasant if unremarkable features and a steady, unimaginative disposition. He leaned back in his chair and frowned. 'Were they happy with the tour?'

'I think so, at least as happy as that pair will ever be. They quarrelled most of the time. I have the distinct impression that I was given conscience money at the end,' she told him with a grimace. 'I'm through for the day, so I might as well go home.'

'Fine. See you tomorrow.' Then, as Kirstie turned to leave, Paul said suddenly, 'Wait a minute. There's a message for you somewhere. I think I have it here on my desk.'

Kirstie froze and inwardly cursed the sudden hammering of her heart. She watched as her brother seemed to take an inordinate amount of time searching through his pile of papers, to emerge with a crumpled slip which he held out to her. She snatched at it and looked at the telephone number written in Paul's large clear script. 'Is that all? Didn't he leave a message?'

'He?' repeated Paul. 'It wasn't a man, it was a woman. Did I forget to write her name down? Helen, I think it was.'

Just as she cursed her wild excitement, so she swore at the leaden sense of disappointment that dragged her mood into depression. Kirstie kept her gaze on the paper for a long moment until she got herself under control, then said flatly, 'I don't know any Helen.'

'Well, give her a call anyway before you leave. It's probably business.'

Kirstie found that the office that Paul's secretary used was empty, so she dialled for an outside line and punched in the number on the slip. After getting an engaged signal on three tries, she gave up, stuffed the number in her pocket and left for home.

That evening she curled into a ball on the couch and watched a weepy movie while eating through the contents of a box of chocolates. Louise breezed out of the house at around seven o'clock, so she knew she could enjoy at least a few hours of solitary peace. She told herself she'd had a good day. She tried to feel pleased at the prospect of spending her fifty dollars. She had just decided to skip the end of the movie and go to bed when the phone in the kitchen shrilled.

Kirstie fell off the couch and ran to answer it. 'Hello?' she said breathlessly before she had the receiver to her ear.

'Did I catch you at a bad time?' murmured familar deep tones.

Francis. She caught her breath, found her voice and lied, 'No, I—was just walking through the front door.'

'I see. Why didn't you return my call today?'

She frowned. 'I didn't get a message that you called.'

'I told my secretary to get in touch with you at the airstrip, but she said you were out.'

Light began to dawn and she asked, 'Is your secretary by any chance named Helen?'

'Yes.'

'I tried to ring her back but the line was engaged.'

'Never mind, I got hold of you in the end. Why don't you come into town and meet me for lunch tomorrow?' he suggested.

Kirstie covered the mouthpiece of her receiver and leaned her forehead against the kitchen wall as she raced through a whole gamut of emotion. Seeing Francis was like playing with a bomb she knew would go off in her face at any time. 'I can't,' she said at last. 'I'm busy tomorrow.'

'Liar,' he told her. 'I talked to your brother Paul earlier, and he said you didn't have anything on for the afternoon.'

Damn him. Damn them both. She screwed up her forehead and tried to think. Francis said silkily, 'We still haven't had our talk.'

'I don't happen to think it's necessary.'

'I do.' He sounded like velvet and iron, and it was a combination she was beginning to dread. 'If you don't want to come into New York, I can always drop by tomorrow evening. I'm sure we can eventually persuade Louise into giving us some privacy.'

'That's blackmail!' she exclaimed, horrified at imagining the scene and furious at him for using such base tactics.

'That's right,' he said serenely. 'See you at one o'clock. You know where the office is. I'll have my secretary reserve a parking space for you.'

'If you think you can coerce me like that——' she shouted, but he had already hung up and she was left gibbering to the high buzz of a dialling tone.

Kirstie slammed the receiver back on the hook and stormed into the empty living-room. How dared he? It would serve him right if she left town, and he came to face Louise alone! It would serve them both right! But then the thought of Louise's cold blue eyes on Saturday morning pulled her up short. Kirstie had no idea what her sister would do if Louise found out she'd been lying.

Perhaps lunch wasn't such a bad idea after all. She could be icy, composed. She could wither Francis with her scorn for his blackmail, intimidate him with her poise. She got a grim sense of satisfaction in contemplating it.

Cripes, she didn't have a thing to wear!

Kirstie did have something to wear by one o'clock on Thursday. She was thankful for it when she walked down the corridor of Amalgamated Trust's executive floor. Original prints adorned the walls; every inch of the patterned grey and steel-blue carpet screamed corporate wealth. The immaculate receptionist downstairs who had given her clearance and directions had looked like a high-class businesswoman. One glance at her and all Kirstie's doubts as to how much she had spent on her appearance had vanished.

Her cream silk blouse, the knee-length tailored beige skirt, the high-heeled pumps became as comforting as a security blanket. Kirstie spoke calmly to Francis's private secretary. When the other woman turned to the intercom, she touched her wide leather belt to make sure it was straight.

The secretary turned back to her with a superbly polished smile. 'I do hope you had a nice drive, Miss Philips. You're welcome to go right in. Can I get you a cup of coffee?'

'No, thank you. There's no need to get up, I'll let myself through.' Kirstie opened one of the double walnut doors and entered Francis's office.

He sat with his head bent over a file at a desk situated in front of a row of windows that reached from ceiling to floor. 'I'm sorry about this, Kirstie. Take a seat, I'll be finished in a minute.'

Tired-looking Francis in that exquisite handmade business suit aroused such a reaction in her that she turned away in silence to study a row of reference books on one of his bookshelves. Her eyes roamed blindly over the leatherbound volumes. Gone was the unscrupulous manipulator from yesterday, and in his place was a man who looked as if he needed nothing more than a hug.

There was a sound of paper shuffling. 'Thank God that's done. If I had to proofread any more statistics, I'd——' He stopped in mid-sentence. Kirstie looked over her shoulder at him. Francis had sat back in his chair, his expression arrested. 'Heavens to Betsy,' he said, 'will you look at that?'

'Hello to you, too,' she said drily and walked over to take the seat across from him. The side slit in the skirt fell apart as she crossed her legs. Francis's green gaze ran up the movement and flared alight. Oh, God, the outfit was a mistake.

He jabbed a button on the console at his right. 'Helen,' he said casually, 'no more calls.'

Kirstie sat straight in her chair. Francis rose to his feet in a leisurely fashion, eyes never leaving her. Blood thundered in her ears. With a brisk gesture she checked her wristwatch. 'Isn't it about time we were leaving?'

He rounded the desk, smiling a lazy, predatory smile. 'There's no hurry.'

She bolted to her feet and whirled in a panic. 'I disagree.' He caught her by the shoulders and turned her back to face him. 'Francis——' she babbled.

'Yes, dear?' he murmured, lifting one hand to run his fingers through the sleek silk of her hair.

All the starch left Kirstie's body in a whoosh. She could have sunk to the floor right there and then. Such a loss of control frightened her; with one touch he broke through every one of her preconceived notions about today and made a mockery of her resolutions. With a panic against that seductive drowning, she fought for coherence. 'I—I'm hungry.'

'So am I,' he whispered, watching her lips. 'You look sensational. In fact, you look more than sensational. You look good enough to eat. Shouldn't we be going?'

His apparent effortless switch from sensuality to practicality had her floundering. She stared at him, stranded in a desert of no reply, and with a groan he put an arm around her shoulders and purposefully steered her out of the door. 'We'll be back around three o'clock, Helen,' he calmly told his secretary.

Kirstie was all too aware of the other woman's fascinated scrutiny as they walked past her desk, but she could do nothing except follow Francis's lead.

He took her down to the garage basement, for her a haunted place. She stayed quiet and subdued under the weight of the terrible memories, meekly getting into the passenger seat of his silver BMW. Francis, however, seemed totally unaffected by the scene. There was no reason for him to be otherwise, as for him the garage was a daily reality and he would have long since exorcised any uncomfortable ghost of the kidnapping.

But that lasting, nagging guilt kept Kirstie preoccupied when another time she might have asked him where they were dining out. Thus they were already pulling up outside the high-rise apartment building by Central Park before she had her wits gathered.

'What's this?' she asked stupidly, as Francis switched off the engine and got out of the car.

He strolled unhurriedly around to her side and opened her door for her, a suppressed smile deepening one corner of his engaging mouth. '"This" is lunch.'

'*Here*?' Shock lent far too much emphasis on the one word that exploded out of her mouth, and she cursed herself furiously as his smile deepened.

'Unless you would prefer that I brought it down to the car?' he asked smoothly. Victor the doorman had approached and stood just behind Francis, so conspicuously not looking at them that Kirstie scrambled out of the car just to avoid having any more of their conversation overheard. Francis carelessly handed over his car keys to the other man while Kirstie twitched her skirt into place with the last tattered remnants of her dignity, then he placed one light hand at the small of her back and escorted her once more up to his apartment.

He'd tricked her. He had deliberately said nothing about this, had manipulated her into coming in the first place—how could she have let her guard down in his office, just because for one heartstopping moment he had looked tired, even inexplicably discouraged? Why couldn't they have gone to a restaurant; why couldn't he have left her barriers intact; what, oh, what was she doing just letting him propel her into his empty private domain? Speculation sent her thinking into a highly erratic skid, so that when they finally entered his apartment, and she saw the sparkling array of crystal, china and heavy cream linen laid out immaculately on his polished dining table, she simply dragged to a halt and stared, speechless.

A delicious scent of freshly baked bread and something that smelled like hollandaise sauce wafted from the kitchen. It was obvious that he had put a lot of thought and planning into this. Francis stood beside her, smiling again at the expression on her face, hands casually tucked in his pockets as he waited until she turned to him with a helpless little shrug. 'I don't know what to say.'

'Must you say anything?' he replied quietly. Her eyes followed the inherent grace of his body as he went to open the balcony door, drawing the curtains to let in the bright afternoon sunlight. 'Why don't you have a seat instead, while I go fetch the soup?'

He left her standing alone, so after a long indecisive moment she surrendered to the occasion and seated herself at the lovely table just as he reappeared carrying a steaming silver tureen. Kirstie peered around his elbow as he served her a generous portion of fresh cream of mushroom soup and then filled his own bowl.

He disappeared again to bring back a crisp French muscadet wine nestled in a sweating ice bucket.

Francis took the seat opposite her, and Kirstie watched the wine he poured splash into her glass. 'How did you arrange all this?' she asked.

He sent her a brilliant, laughing glance, the green of his eyes the vivid focal point of the entire room. 'I stayed up half the night cooking?'

'Don't tease,' she begged in a mutter, her own grey eyes falling back to her soup as she tasted it. It was, she found without surprise, superb.

'I have this fairy godmother,' said Francis, relenting as he settled back in his seat with a sigh of relaxation. Bit by bit the marks of pressure he had been wearing like war wounds in the office eased away. The difference was so remarkable that it took years off his face. 'Her name, you may remember from your last visit here, is Mrs Callihan. She cleans, does the shopping and cooks whenever I need it. I do believe that if I asked her she would tuck me into bed at night with a hot toddy.'

'You're lucky,' she said, savouring the rich, delicate flavour of her soup.

'I know it. It is no exaggeration, believe me, when I say I don't know how I'd have survived these last five years without her.'

Something in his expression caught her attention, not so much the words, as he had spoken so very indifferently. Giving in to impulse, she laid down her spoon and asked, as she stared at her empty bowl, 'Francis, how do you stand it?'

He didn't pretend to misunderstand, or prevaricate. Instead, he replied with a quiet straightforwardness that was made all the more terrible by the very lack of self-pity. 'Oh, I was young and ambitious, and work was just a game I wanted to win. I had all the time in the world and so, like the rich, I squandered it. Then working all day became just a habit, far easier to continue when I had made no outside emotional investment. It's a very common occurrence.'

'But what about the things that can enrich you so much?' she asked, aching at thought of the dry existence he depicted with such intimate knowledge. 'What about a family, friends, children?'

'Now there's a question,' he said, and by acknowledging it with such wry adroitness turned it neatly aside. He looked up and sent her a little twisted smile. 'Time for the main course, I think.'

He took away the used tableware and brought in an outstanding entrée of freshly steamed salmon steaks with creamed broccoli and new potatoes, refilled her wine glass and lifted his glass to her in a mocking salute. 'To my kidnapper,' he toasted, raising his eyebrows in amusement when she sat as still as stone.

'I won't drink to that,' she said abruptly, turning her face aside, breathing hard against a sudden constriction in her chest.

'No? A pity, as it was the most—interesting thing that has happened to me in some time.' Her face flamed over with mortification as he drank deeply from his glass, then said, still in that careless, frivolous way of his, 'And really, I can't think of a better way for you to get rid of that persistent guilt of yours, which is about as much use to carry around as a fifth wheel.'

'I acted wrongly on wrong information,' she stated flatly, spearing a flake of her salmon without making any effort to eat it. She stared at it, her eyes too heavy, too reluctant to meet his. 'You didn't deserve it, Francis.'

'No?' he repeated, and again the word was a question. She frowned and opened her mouth to pursue it, but he forestalled her with another question. 'Tell me, would you still have done it to someone who did, as you say, deserve it?'

That brought her eyes up, large and revealingly bewildered as she replied with difficulty, 'I—probably not. My thinking has—changed too much. I'm no longer quite so arrogant.'

'Funnily enough,' he said, so lightly, holding her eyes, 'neither am I. Kirstie, if other people are prepared to forgive you for your mistakes, don't you think you can learn to forgive yourself?'

Hearing that mellifluous voice of his shape her name, as always, felt as if he pulled her out of herself. The compelling sensation flared in her eyes an instant before she parried his penetrating observances with a question of her own. 'What makes you think I haven't already?'

'I know too well how you are ruthless with yourself, far more so than with others. You make allowances for people that you refuse to make for yourself. It was only because you thought I was so reprehensible that you felt compelled to do something. Would you like dessert?' he asked, with another of those disconcerting switches of subject.

Brought back to the present, she found, to her surprise, that her meal was completely gone. 'Er—no, thank you.'

'Coffee, then?'

'Yes, please.'

She began to gather her silverware together and was detained by his warm, firm grasp on her wrist. 'No, leave it. I told you: I have this fairy godmother, and she's getting paid overtime to come in this evening.

You wouldn't want to do the lady out of her gambling money, would you?'

Kirstie had to laugh at that and let the silverware remain in its place, while Francis went back to the kitchen to brew a pot of coffee. She was left alone, and the room around her settled into silence.

Don't you think you can learn to forgive yourself?

Kirstie stood slowly, and slowly she turned towards the hot sunlight shining on the balcony. She stepped out and leaned against the solid concrete waist-high wall to look down at the street below. Distant honks and traffic noises wafted up; more real were the flocks of birds that perched on and swooped from power lines, and the tops of the trees in Central Park.

Francis had spoken with keener wisdom than perhaps he knew. Even their differing reactions to the basement garage pointed to it. He didn't need her guilt, nor did he want it. He had as much as said so. She couldn't eradicate what had happened by carrying it with her wherever she went. It was indeed time to let it go, time to stop trying to make amends.

It was also time to stop fooling herself, for, if guilt had been her crutch, so too had it been the easiest, most acceptable reason for agreeing to see Francis again. She had never dealt properly with how devastating she found him to her self-control and self-containment. She was drawn to him, sexually, intellectually and emotionally, and had been even back as early as the time spent in Vermont. It was the most powerful pull towards another human being she had ever experienced, and the implications tumbling outwards from that realisation alone frightened her to death.

CHAPTER NINE

SHE sensed him before she heard him, standing silently at the open balcony door behind her, and with a quick reflexive turn of her head she saw that she had caught him off guard.

Reaction tumbled inwards and broke barriers. She wanted to say to him, This was an accident. You weren't supposed to see what was in my eyes, just as I never meant to surprise that look in yours.

Her gaze was wide and wondering, like a child's. His was patient. A breeze caught the light curtains in the doorway and moulded it over half his torso and one shoulder, and as he moved forward it slid rippling away.

He covered the distance between them in quiet, contained steps. One of his hands came under her chin and cradled the fragile shape, and he tilted her face up. His eyes roamed each sculptured bone, touched her own grey gaze in a question, became fixated on her mouth. He started to bend his head.

He never rushed her; he never hurried. Kirstie had blundered along the entire wild range of emotions throughout his languid movements, from startlement, to fear, to flinching anxiety. Now his impossible deliberation shattered her resolve. There was nowhere for her to turn, no form of steadfast principle, nothing to override the compulsion. She tumbled into blind action, wound both arms around his neck, pulled his head down the rest of the way and offered him her mouth.

Francis's composure disintegrated. A groan pierced his body, and with unthinking need he clutched her hips to haul her against him. Her knees malfunctioned. She gave into desire and moulded herself to the hard, curved support of his strong body. His hands ran up her back, their urgent pressure wrecking the neat, tucked-in blouse, which came free from her belt and let him explore the contours and hollows of her flesh. His tongue stroked hers with eager tenderness, then he gnawed, concentrated and delicate, on the full, sensitive curve of her bottom lip.

Her craving turned rabid. She shuddered down her entire length and let her head fall to his shoulder.

He broke from the luscious ravishment of her lips to dive down the angle of her neck and tease aside the collar of her blouse. He felt as if he had a fever. He felt and reacted as if this had never happened to him before, as if all the other times they had come together in physical need had never been, as if this were the first, the most precious, the only time of his life.

She turned her face into his gleaming black hair and hardly noticed as he peeled open the buttons of her blouse with trembling, barely restrained care. Then the blouse fell open and for the tirst time he feasted upon the slight curve of her small breasts, and the quiet, heartfelt sound that came from him then sent her arcing in instinctive reaction into the soft caress of his hands.

She was lost, so lost, melting into the flaming sensation of liquid pleasure that flickered as his fingers flickered, across her tight pink nipples, coursing through her body. She gasped as, with one muscle-flexing surge, he wrapped one powerful arm around her slender waist and lifted her effortlessly up so that his hungry mouth could nip, and suckle, and stroke across her breasts.

It was an exquisite, voluptuous agony that couldn't last. Pleasure combined with an ache in her lower back, caused by the strain of their postures, but still she willed the moment never to end, as she bowed head and shoulders over his own bent head and held his face against her. When at last he had to let her sink slowly back until her feet touched the ground, her body slid hard along the quivering length of his so that they both cried out in mutual loss, and he drowned it away in the excesses of yet another explorative kiss.

Yes, she was lost, careening wildly through a smoky labyrinth towards a molten core, recognising at last the nature of the compulsion which disregarded creed, barriers, life—called love.

No. In her heart and in her head she said it.

An echo of the whisper, hoarsely, from Francis, still trapped in the labyrinth, 'Do you have any idea how long it's been since I have made love to a woman?'

'Oh, God!' she cried, in deepest torment. Made love?

No.

'I want to suck you slowly,' he muttered in her ear. 'I want to bury myself in you so deeply I'll never come out. I want to pull you on top of me, take hold of your thighs——'

'Stop it!' Pain, to stop it. She struggled against the tidal wave and panted, despairingly, 'Oh, Francis, it isn't right!'

His head jerked back, as if he were a puppet on a string. Was he too far gone to hear the voice of reason?

It isn't right until it is made right.

There was too much that was uncertain, undefined, and too much of herself was at stake. If they drank now, heedless of all else in their lives, what they partook of could well turn to poison, and she didn't know if they could survive it. Meaning to push him away, she brought her hands to his chest. By some inexplicable accident, by her own inherent weakness, when they touched him they stroked taut, shirt-covered muscles.

His whole body shuddered. He grasped her hands so hard that the bones ground together. 'God *don't do that*!' he cried. 'I have about as much control right now as a fifteen-year-old virgin!'

Control was what she was striving for. Dark colour suffused her cheeks, then left her dizzy with desertion and marble-cold, marble-white. She dragged away from his bruising grip and fumbled to put her clothing to rights, shakily tucking her blouse into place. 'This isn't right,' she forced out, parrot-like.

The balcony, the air, even the birds were still. 'Why isn't it?' he asked very quietly.

'This—this preoccupation,' she began.

'Quite an interesting euphemism,' he said, and the mocking, angry taunt was so accurate, hurt so much, that her eyes flashed hot diamond at him.

'Would you prefer that I call it *corrosive obsession*?' she lashed, and as it whipped across his face she saw that she had given every bit as much hurt as she had sustained. 'If we sink into this, we won't be dealing with issues, we will be ignoring basic problems. . .'

His restraint now was total; he had what she had tried for and had failed to achieve: control. 'What are the problems?' Again, very quietly.

'Our lives!' She was too wrapped up in her own agitation to notice how silken he had gone, and to remember how dangerous that quality of his was. 'What about Louise?'

'Ah, yes. Louise again,' he murmured, and the silk-covered glove struck. 'We must always remember to consider her thoughts and her feelings. After all, looking after Louise is one of the things you do best, isn't it?'

'What?' Kirstie turned back to him, and she retreated a step under the sight of his volcanic fury.

'What kind of life do you have, anyway?' he snarled. 'Or do you have one at all, that's more to the point! Perhaps you get your kicks vicariously by watching Louise's dramas! And when she crooks her little finger or throws a tantrum you just go running back! It's such a good excuse for not venturing out on your own, isn't it?'

Francis, watching, had not thought it possible for her to go even whiter, but she did, and said between rage-stiffened lips, 'How dare you attack me like that? You know nothing about my life, nothing!'

'No?' Francis leaned back against the stone support of the balcony wall. 'It looks like a pretty clear picture from where I'm standing.'

'In fact,' Kirstie said, succinct away from that sensual, riotous confusion, 'I'm beginning to wonder if you know anything at all. My consideration for Louise is irrefutable, but do you still think that I am the same blindly loyal person I was in Vermont. Yes, I would protect her from malice, but I would also protect myself from her malice. She is, after all, a fact of my life, and only one of many. Did you think you could have me, now, without all that entails? And was I supposed to fall into your bed just this once, regardless of the future, your responsibilities, your work that you have made your life?'

His attack had brought no tears; it had, after all, been reaction to her own ungentle disentanglement.

But now, as realisation left him visibly stricken, she found her cheeks grow wet. 'It isn't right until it is made right. It isn't even yet a matter of what the answers are, but what the questions are, and each of us getting our priorities straight.'

Passion, fury, that brief contempt had died. Keeping well away from her—not a retreat, she knew, but a conscious consideration—Francis said, his eyes very dark, 'Of course you're right. Please forgive me.'

But she shook her head in denial and whispered, 'We hurt each other.'

He moved, made as if to speak, and the tears still fell sparkling from the ever-changing grey of her eyes, for she knew that this was the moment he, in possession of his mind and not his senses, would either retreat forever or take that first fateful step forward, and, God help her, she did not know if she had the strength to face his retreat.

The telephone in the living-room shrilled, shockingly obnoxious in the charged, waiting atmosphere. They both stared at each other, rigid, and Francis turned his head aside to spit a curse with soft vehemence. He strode through the open balcony door, snatched up the phone receiver, bit out, 'Yes?' then snapped, 'I told you I wasn't to be disturbed! As far as the office is concerned, I'm still at lunch! I don't damned well care if it is Tokyo—oh, for God's sake! All right—all right! I'll take the call here!' He hung up and turned to look at her framed in the doorway, his expression bleak. 'I have to take this call.'

It was not such a blow after all, merely cold. Kirstie felt the winter ice spread through her body and knew that she hadn't expected anything else. She said quietly, 'I quite understand.'

Some spark of vitality had been extinguished in her,

leaving a shell of a woman behind, and Francis frowned at the change in her. 'I don't think you do.'

Her smile was faint. It did not reach her eyes. She looked at him clearly, wryly. 'In the end, does it really matter?'

The phone rang again, and he glared at it. All the pressure, all the tension had lined him again with the wounds of his unforgiving game. Kirstie's smile then reached her eyes, her wryness turned on herself. Corrosive obsession, indeed. How could she have entertained the hope that there might be room for her as well? 'Answer your phone call, Francis,' she urged him gently.

He picked up the receiver, spoke into it. She gathered her bag off the floor by the couch where she had left it, and walked out of his apartment.

'Wait!' Francis shouted, and, if she had but seen it, this was the harshest blow she had dealt him yet. He hesitated just that instant too long, then slammed the receiver down and raced flat out for the lift down the hall. The doors were closing, and Kirstie's eyes were covered by one hand. She didn't see him. Though he knew it was useless, he continued to the gleaming metal doors, placed his hands on them, and after a long moment bent his head.

Then he straightened, turned with terrible composure and walked back to his apartment, glitteringly beautiful and not merely empty but desolate. The phone was ringing again. After a thoughtful moment, he sighed and picked it up. Then after a lengthy, statistic-oriented conversation, he checked the time and made a few more phone calls.

Get your priorities right.

*   *   *

Kirstie sat at the breakfast table on Friday morning, her exhausted head in her arms. She had weathered the storm of doubt and regret, and now felt empty, drained of everything but conviction. All her whirling confusion had been burned to ash by the passage of the night, spent in unsleeping torment with improvident disregard for her own stamina. By some extraordinary sense, she thought at times that she could touch Francis's own restless conjecturings, his unstinting search for the truth to his own needs.

Had she moved too fast, had the conclusions she jumped to yesterday been, by any chance, wrong? She didn't think so. Walking out on Francis had not been an act of pique for the moment, but one of clear-sighted ruthlessness, forgoing all the heartbreaking discussion and drawn-out pain.

By leaving him she had shown that she would not accept second place, and would not, out of consideration for him, beg or coerce anything out of him that he was not willing to give. Could he change? Could he lessen the all-consuming demand on his time, thinking and life to make room for tenderness? Just as importantly, could he do so without future reproach?

She didn't know. She couldn't guess whether the phone would some day ring for her, and had to exist, for the sake of her own sanity, without hope, for hope without realisation was unbearable.

Her own priorities had fallen into crystalline simplicity yesterday with that instant, awesome recognition of the depth of her love for him. Love, more potent than passion, more considerate than selfishness, had broken that consuming fever and brought her to peace at last.

She would give him anything, even if what he needed most was nothing at all.

The sun was rising; at long last the night was over.

She called, out of the depth of her exhaustion, for endurance and somewhere, somehow, found it. Life went on, even after revelations that brought one to a standstill. There were duties to be performed, there was work to be done, and after a shoulder-shaking sigh Kirstie rose from her seat and made coffee.

Distantly she heard the sounds of the shower running and knew that Louise would be down shortly for breakfast, and the start of her day. Louise, beautiful and dangerous, had always known far better than she how to survive. She found it in her heart to pity simple, kind-hearted Neil who had fallen in love with Louise only to be slashed to the quick.

Her sister had gone out last night, glittering with glamour and illicit excitement. Kirstie had already been locked in the silent privacy of her bedroom and so had not witnessed Louise's whirlwind return to the house, though she'd heard it in the emphatic slam of the front door, and other sounds that heralded the climactic end of either a successful evening or disaster. Louise's reaction to both ecstasy and fury were the same, violent in nature and tempestuous.

Kirstie knew she was about to face the aftermath, and braced her weary self for Louise's entry half an hour later.

'Good morning,' she said quietly, as behind her the kitchen door swung open. She reached into a cupboard for a mug. 'Would you like a cup of coffee?'

'Yes, please!' replied Louise briskly. Kirstie poured it and turned, halting for a moment at the picture before her.

For Louise that morning was staggering. Dressed in a stunning outfit of royal blue and high-heeled pumps, her lustrous blonde hair twisted into an elegant knot that emphasised a long, tempting neck and heart-shaped face, each feature delicately, artistically tinted with tasteful make-up, she wore her beauty like a burnished tiara, hard, jewelled and sparkling.

Kirstie set the coffee carefully on the kitchen table, while Louise stalked towards the refrigerator and pulled out orange juice, then turned back to smile at her with blue, charged eyes. 'Well?' murmured her sister. 'How do I look?'

'Fantastic,' replied Kirstie simply, well aware that she herself wore her disruptive night like a shabby cloak. She sat down and unashamedly stared. 'That's quite an outfit for high-school chemistry.'

Louise threw back her head, exposing her long white throat, and laughed. 'This isn't for the doubtful benefit of my chemistry classes!' she exclaimed, and the amusement was in her voice as well, tinkling like shards of splintered glass. 'This is for my lunch date today. I'm going out with that incredibly sexy man you kidnapped with such good intentions.'

Everything in Kirstie stopped.

She had not been at a standstill before. How long would she continue to deceive herself, how much more was there to strip away and learn? She had been in limbo, refusing to give up that last tiny ember of hope, refusing even to fan it to a flame, sheltering it from all else that crumbled to ash. But she couldn't shelter it from the cutting presence facing her now.

Slashed.

She moved finally, and from memory aped a normal expression, an unremarkable surprise. 'This is an—unexpected development,' she said, while those hot blue eyes tried remorselessly to dissect her façade.

'Oh, not really,' declaimed Louise airily, settling herself with ineffable grace into the seat opposite her.

She was too close. Kirstie felt it like an outcry jammed at the back of her throat. 'I'd been in touch, you see, after the wedding had been cancelled, but Francis had been really too busy the first couple of weeks to socialise, poor man. However, he called me yesterday, we got together last night, and—well, the rest, as they say, is history. By the way, don't expect me in for supper tonight. I expect we'll celebrate with a night on the town.'

'How very nice.' Kirstie murmured the senseless words, picked up her coffee and took a sip of it without any of it registering. Could she breathe past the pain in her chest; did she? She must have, for this cruel consciousness continued.

Slashed to the quick.

With an excess of good will, Louise leaned forward and captured one of her cold, lifeless hands. 'Whether you know it or not, you've done us an incredible favour,' said her older sister, with her characteristic impeccable charm. 'If you hadn't shaken us both up by what you'd done, I might have gone ahead and married Neil, while Francis would have just stepped aside with that typical generosity of his, and we all would have been utterly miserable right now. But instead, you gave us each the shock we needed to make us put our lives right, and we owe it all to you.'

'You don't owe me anything,' said Kirstie through motionless lips, and Louise, unsurprised, smiled.

'And how typical of you too, darling. Oh, God, look at the time!' She swept, cat-smooth and sinuous, to her feet and carried her empty cup to the sink. 'By the way,' Louise continued, with such an enchanting mixture of embarrassment and delight, 'is it possible for you to do me another tremendous favour? If you aren't already planning to go out this evening, do you think you could absent yourself from the living-room so that I can bring him back for coffee—afterwards? I'll lug the television up to your bedroom if you like.'

'No, that—won't be necessary,' she whispered, through a rising wave of nausea. She couldn't bear being in the same house with them together. 'I have a feeling I'll be working this evening.'

'You are a love!' Louise danced over and brushed her cheek against Kirstie's, so as not to smudge her lipstick. 'I really must run now, or I'll be late for class! Bye!'

The tremors began as Louise's light, energetic foot-steps tapped towards the front door. By the time the house was shrouded in emptiness, Kirstie's hands and face had crumbled into despair. It was so unimportant, only a physical manifestation of the ruin inside. No one was even around to see it, yet the feeling was so naked, she cradled her body against it.

Get your priorities right, Francis.

It was such supreme irony, to think that she had worried for him more than she'd worried for herself. She had underestimated Francis to the very end. He had taken her advice to the fullest extent, and his clear-sighted ruthlessness had far and above out-stripped hers.

She could see the rationale behind it, and it was faultless. There could not be a better choice of one materialistic enough to disregard his long working hours for the benefits of living such a luxurious life-style. No compromise was necessary with Louise, who was so adroit at looking after herself that he needn't bother. Lavish her with credit cards and champagne, adorn her with jewellery and furs, and she would never be jealous of his true mistress, would play sexuality for a sometime game and not give it undue importance, would preen in the hostess role.

Oh, Francis.

Kirstie mourned for what might have been, what would never be hers, with the knowledge that, as with her guilt, as with her protectiveness, he neither needed her love nor wanted it.

Then, as there was nothing else for her to do, she washed her face and dressed, her body jerking tiredly through the meaningless motions. She packed an overnight bag, for she was desperate to keep the distance between herself and what was to happen in this house. Perhaps Christian might be persuaded to put her up for the night, and this weekend she would scour the newspapers for a small apartment she could take closer to the airstrip.

And in the meantime she would go and work herself past exhaustion, where there was still this appalling pain, to a barren state where nothing could exist, where the passage of the night went unremarked in destitute slumber. And when the next day dawned she would do it again. Some travesty of life went on, even after the most debilitating revelations.

She knew intellectually that somewhere, some time after the test of endurance, she would stop hurting so much inside. She might even be able to meet Francis, with his arm around her sister, and smile. Adults were like that. But for now she couldn't help crying a little for the appalling pain that existed.

CHAPTER TEN

'CHRISTIAN'S a no-show,' said Paul wearily just after lunch. With an uncharacteristic display of temper he threw a clipboard with the day's schedule off his desk. It hit the tiled floor with a resounding slap. 'Damn his unpredictable hide.'

Kirstie sat in his office with a peculiar quiet as if she had abandoned her body, her expressionless eyes watching her eldest brother. Her face looked as if it had been cut from unkind stone, the planes and hollows under her eyes and cheeks chiselled without the redeeming quality of colour. None of her customary mischievous bounce was in evidence; it was as if a totally different personality had taken her over. Occasionally throughout the morning people asked if she was feeling all right, to which she replied with a courtesy made hideous with the lack of sincerity, emotion, any normal human reaction.

Now what she said in response to Paul was, 'Don't judge him too harshly. He's never skipped out without some kind of warning before. There must be a reason for his absence.'

'Oh, I know,' replied Paul, expelling a short, impatient sigh. 'But that doesn't get cargo shipped, and if we don't meet the deadline we could lose a two-hundred-thousand-a-year contract.'

Kirstie swung around in her swivel-chair and rubbed tired eyes. 'I'll take it.'

An unusual silence met her offer. She looked up as it registered, found Paul watching her with doubt. 'Are you sure you're up to it?' he asked, and the gentle concern was so weakening that she gripped the arms of her seat until the bones in her hands showed stark.

'I'm up to it.'

He didn't give it up. 'The latest reports say that the weather is going to worsen. There'll be no room for sloppy flying.'

That brought the first real sign of emotion from her: anger. 'You know better than that. I have never flown a sloppy flight in my life,' she gritted, eyes flashing.

'I know,' he replied softly. 'You're one of the best pilots I've got. But I've never seen you look the way you do today, and I don't want there to be a first time for you. You know the schedule as well as I. There's no other available pilot. But I'd rather sacrifice the contract than have you at any risk.'

It brought her up short, as it was meant to. She considered her own resources again, running through the length and demands of the flight with a new objectivity, while Paul sat and waited. At the end she shook her head and gave him a brief, pale smile. 'I'm down but I'm not foolish. My flying won't be a risk.'

'Fine,' he said, with an encouraging nod, and turned back to his work. 'Be ready to leave at two o'clock.'

Kirstie stood. 'Who'll stay tonight to see me in?'

'I will.' Paul didn't look up.

She hesitated, something niggling at her memory. 'I thought you had Carol's parents coming tonight?'

Her brother glanced at her from under raised eyebrows. 'I'll stay to see you in, Kirstie.' It could have been a rebuff. Paul was capable of it, if he felt his authority was being challenged. But they both knew she hadn't meant the question to be a challenge, and the warm, caring smile he gave her was an altogether different message.

Paul, too, had his share of family loyalty.

She quietly shut the door behind her. At her emergence, his secretary told her, 'I've another message for you, Kirstie.'

It was the second one that day. Kirstie didn't want to talk to anyone and replied, 'I'm still not in. Whoever it is can wait until Monday.'

Routine was soothing. She checked her flight path and the cargo, already loaded, initialled the inventory list, and listened to another weather report with Paul before setting off. Thunderstorms were due to eclipse New Jersey in the early hours of the morning. Briefly, to cover all contingencies, they discussed the possibility of her staying overnight in Cincinnati and decided it wasn't necessary. She would have a gusty return, but she should be touching down well before the storm would break. On that note, she took her leave.

The day seemed so unreal. After a month of unrelieved heat the grey sky felt strange, and the distant place inside where she had hidden her real self had nothing to do with lifting the plane off the runway, or with taxiing into the large hangar at Cincinnati so that the ground crew there could unload the cargo sheltered from lashing sheets of rain.

She waited patiently while everything that could go wrong did, from an accident with a forklift to a miscount on the inventory so that everything had to be checked again. Kirstie didn't mind, because it didn't touch her. It was all surface noise, a comforting distraction, and when business had been concluded, hours behind schedule, she made the decision to continue home late that evening without regret, for to stop at that point meant she might fall victim to wounding reflection.

She hadn't known at that time that the storm was

moving in much faster than had previously been indicated, nor that the head-winds would give her lightened aircraft a constant buffeting, making the autopilot useless and scoring tension along her wrists and shoulders. She was more than halfway home before she hit the worst of it, and by then turning back was no longer an option.

Reaction she had been fleeing from struck her at the darkest point, when the violent wind was her only companion. She was lonely, so lonely, she was tired and aching and utterly discouraged. She couldn't remember why she should want to return, ever, her lack of direction was total, and the silent sobs clenched her chest as she mechanically refused to let tears destroy her vision.

It was approaching midnight by the time she could contact Paul through the interference to tell him she was over the Appalachian Mountains and in the home stretch. For a moment she thought she had lost him again, but then he said, eloquent with feeling, 'My God. There you are.'

She heard it, and understood, for her enforced radio silence had stretched to over an hour in which, to Paul and the skeletal ground crew waiting helpless at the airstrip, anything could have happened. Out of the modicum of pity left in her destitute emotions, she sent him, briefly, the only reassurance she could. 'Not long now, Paul. I'll see you soon.'

It was fifteen minutes later, as she was bringing the plane down through the storm by sheer determination to the lighted runway, that it happened. The wicked, capricious wind hurled itself at the light plane just a few feet from touching ground, and she knew, as she fought savagely for control, that nothing—Paul's earlier concern, a fresher pilot—could have prevented it.

The right wheels connected with the drenched asphalt and screamed a protest for over a hundred hair-raising yards, the sole support for the weight of the careening plane as she did all that she could to keep it from turning on its side.

There was so much noise, but inside there was nothing, just the shudder of the aircraft and one second of immense relief as at last it obeyed her commands and righted itself. She was still braking as hard as she dared when the overstressed right side of the landing-gear collapsed.

Kirstie felt a violent jerk as her seat fell out from underneath her. She watched the black wet ground come up to meet her. The underside of the plane impacted with the landing-strip with an awesome roar, and skidded, slewed sideways over the lighted boundary. One hearbeat, a crashing thud, loudest of all. Two heartbeats. When would the plane stop?

Now. Blessed cessation.

It stopped just now.

Hanging sideways in her seat-straps, numb all over with shock, Kirstie closed her eyes and bowed her head forward, and found herself apologising with heartbreaking dejection, 'Oh, Paul. I'm so sorry.'

'Jesus. *Jesus* Christ!' The radio was still operable and open, Paul a horrified witness to the whole ghastly incident. But then she knew that. The abused metal hadn't been the only scream to ravish her ears.

Then there was silence, and the wet-lashed darkness. She had no energy for disentangling herself, passively waiting for the screech of tyres, the shouts, the urgent assault upon the exterior of the crazily tilted plane. The small door to her cabin was wrenched open almost off its hinges.

She turned her head. *Christian*? With gentle, shaking

fingers her big blond brother quickly unstrapped her. 'Oh, love, where are you hurt?' he cried.

'I—don't think I am,' she said, looking so small in the dim reflected light from the control panel, sounding so uncertain that he wrapped both arms around her and held her with his whole body.

He lifted her out, staggering for secure footing, and walked up the angle of the floor to the open hatch. There Grandpa Whit waited with wiry arms outstretched to take her from Christian and, like him, hug her close convulsively.

She was wet to the skin almost immediately. Someone shook out a blanket and wrapped it around her torso. The rest of the ground crew raced around the plane, spraying it with foam against the possibility of fire, the hissing sound like the release of a pressure cooker. Christian swung lightly out of the plane to the ground. Another speeding ground car approached the scene as she turned her head and said shakily, 'Grandpa, I can walk.'

'Are you sure, girl?' he asked as he cuddled her, but he was already lowering her legs carefully to the ground.

At that moment the other ground car screeched to a halt and two dark figures exploded out of it. Two men sprinting, one of whom was Paul.

The other, faster one was Francis.

Her legs were the first to go, collapsing from underneath her. With a harsh exclamation, her grandfather clutched her as she went to her knees, a loud roar filling her ears. She stared up at Francis with blank eyes gone as large as an owl's as he pulled his body to a precipitate halt, his eyes stark, his face so raw, so exposed in the uneven flash of siren lights from the ground crew's vehicles.

He opened his mouth, said nothing, and sank to his knees in front of her. With delicate hunger, he reached out and gathered her body to him as she fell finally from all that was inexplicable, all that hurt, into darkness.

'I couldn't,' she said, though she didn't know it. 'Paul, I couldn't help it.'

'I know,' said the man holding her, and the two words were a loving croon. 'There was nothing you could do. We saw it all happen, love. God help us, we saw it all.'

Kirstie was conscious enough to be aware of being laid, tenderly, on to something that felt like a couch. There were lights, shining red, on the other side of her closed lids. Her body felt funny, thick. She opened her eyes.

And looked into emerald ones.

She just lay there staring at him, on the couch in Paul's office. Francis made a convulsive movement towards her, and with despair she shrank into herself, for one touch from him and she would fall into so many pieces that she would never pull together again.

He saw, in that split second. She couldn't have stopped him more effectively if she had punched him in the stomach. He recoiled, and his eyes went dead.

Then Paul crouched in front of her with a cup of coffee. 'I've called the doctor,' he said, with such extreme care that she knew he was holding on to the bare threads of his common sense.

'Paul,' she said gently, clearly, for in that moment she was stronger than he, 'I don't need a doctor. I didn't even bang my head. I fainted because I was so tired, and I had a bad scare. Call him up and tell him not to come.'

'Are you sure?' he asked, wanting to be reassured.

'Yes.' Then, as her mouth and voice wobbled, she whispered, 'All I want to do is go h-home.'

It pulled Paul together more efficiently than anything else could have. Suddenly he was in control, still concerned but capable, and he touched her face. 'Then you shall,' he said simply.

'You've got things to take care of here, and she's in no condition to drive,' said Francis in a quiet voice. 'I'll take her.'

Kirstie's eyes flashed to him, fearful, uncomprehending of why he was here at all, but he wasn't looking at her. He was looking instead at Paul, who nodded his relief at the suggestion. Then, as Francis made an impersonal gesture as if he would help her rise, she quickly struggled to her feet while pretending she hadn't seen.

Paul hugged and kissed her, then looked deep into her eyes and said, 'It wasn't your fault. You know that, don't you? It was as if a giant hand had picked the plane up. It was incredible you were able to bring it back to ground at all.'

God help us, we saw it all. In that moment she remembered it being said, in torment, and by whom, and she covered her eyes, overcome. Then, to spare her anything further, her brother said gently, 'I'll call you tomorrow and come to see you on Sunday. Go get some sleep now, hm?'

Kirstie nodded. After a hesitation, receiving silent affirmation from Francis that she didn't see, Paul patted her shoulder and left them alone.

The storm sounded outside, a low, ominous rumble. She had let her hand fall lifelessly to her side but still could not look up at Francis, who asked, after a moment, 'Are you steady enough to walk to the car?'

Her control was precarious enough that another expression of concern would have ruined her. But he spoke so matter-of-factly that she nodded again and found it true. He matched her slow pace, and waited by the passenger door until she was settled within before going around the other side and climbing in himself.

He didn't try to talk. He just drove sedately through the quiet neighbourhood streets, turning on the heat to warm her, and she found in the silence room to think of all that puzzled her about that evening, until the one question that overrode everything was, 'Why?'

'Why what?' he asked, and turned on to her street.

'Why were you there this evening?' Kirstie turned her head and looked at him.

Other than mildly raising his eyebrows, he looked tired but composed. From all that was shown in his expression, the little scene in Paul's office might never have happened. 'For the same reason,' he replied after a moment, and his face changed, and she knew it all had happened, every bit, 'I came to the airstrip the first time, and called you so many times today. Because, my dear, I cannot stay away.'

She broke down, after all, and sobbed, '*Dear God*, why can't you make up your mind between the two of us?'

The car, neatly and with swift control, pulled to one side. He flicked off the engine and turned to take her by the shoulders with both hard hands. 'I don't understand you. Tell me what you mean, Kirstie,' he said, urgent and contained.

'Louise,' whispered Kirstie. 'You want Louise.'

'I wouldn't touch Louise with a ten-foot pole.' The desperation in his face was too much to take, and two tears spilled out of her swimming eyes.

'She told me you did. You saw her.'

He sucked in his breath harshly with the shock of it, then said with quiet savagery, 'God damn her for a lying, vicious bitch.'

And he twisted to fling open his door. Kirstie realised at last that she was home, but her eyes were only on Francis, as he raced through the rain to her front door and slammed his fist into it twice. Then, impelled by fear for the violence thrumming through his entire body, she scrambled out of the car and ran towards him as the door opened and Louise, casual in jeans and sweater, looked at him with animosity and taunted, 'She isn't here, Francis. She's spending the night somewhere else—with whom, I don't know.'

Kirstie stumbled to a stop just behind Francis's left shoulder, her mind ripped open by the malice in what her sister had just uttered, and Louise saw her for the first time.

Francis put out one hand and pushed Louise aside. The other woman staggered as he brushed past her, rampaged through the ground floor and found a bag. As Kirstie crept across the threshold dumbly, a stunned spectator, her sister spat a curse and lunged for her property, but he had already ripped it open, looked inside the wallet, seen money, Louise's driving licence and car keys.

Francis turned to Louise, his expression frightening. Even she shrank back as he reached for her, but he merely grabbed her by the arm, forcibly marched her to the door and flung her out, and the bag after her. He towered in the doorway, while just beyond him Kirstie could see Louise sprawled on the lawn, her hair flattened by the rain, every vestige of beauty erased by the vile expression on her face.

'Get out,' enunciated Francis flatly. 'Get out of here, or I will kill you.'

Dear God, dear God. Both women, looking at him, fully believed that he would. Louise scrambled gracelessly to her feet, snatched her bag up and ran for her car. Kirstie backed away, groped for the armchair behind her and sank into it.

Francis slammed the door shut and threw on its chain. Then he leaned against it and buried his face in his hands. She watched his chest shudder as he gulped in great swallows of air.

She murmured, tentatively, 'Francis?'

A blind movement of his head to the sound of her frightened voice. 'I saw her,' he said from between his teeth, raggedly. 'Last night. I told her about us. I told her I loved you. I thought I could spare you that.' After a moment the terrifying fury had ebbed enough so that he could bare his face, and he leaned his head back against the door, concluding drily with a masterful understatement, 'It is obvious she didn't take it very well.'

'Love me?' she whispered.

He looked at her, his eyes dark and open, and without defence of any kind. 'Love you,' he said. 'Yes. Since Vermont. Since that long ago, and more each time I see you. Completely and forever.' He took a shuddering breath and averted his head from her astonishment. 'I had not meant to tell you in such a way.'

Her hand raised, went out to him, but of course he couldn't see. Kirstie said to him then, vibrantly, 'But I am so glad that you did tell me, for you see, I thought I loved you alone.'

And all delight sprang afresh from the face that he turned to her, and he was new.

A ring. It was too much, the last straw, it was, unbelievably at that time of night, the phone. Kirstie ran to it, lifted the receiver up and without listening to who was on the other end snapped, 'Buzz off!'

An incoherent sound exploded from Francis. He was, as she whipped around, holding his sides and shaking. Beside herself with concern, she took several steps towards him, then stood in a quandary of confusion, as she saw that he was not in tears but rich in laughter.

But Francis knew what to do. He strode forward lightly, held out his welcoming arms, and with a rush she was in them and held, and was held back as laughter died and fervency drove his lips to hers, to brush, to devour, to search and supplicate.

He broke at last from that engagement and buried his face convulsively into her neck, tasting, crushing, cradling, and his whole strong body trembled. 'You walked out on me yesterday, and I thought of never seeing you again,' he whispered. 'I couldn't stand it. And when I thought I was watching you die tonight I knew I was watching myself die as well.'

'But I didn't,' she murmured as she nuzzled him, urgent to get him away from that raw place. 'Louise devastated me this morning, and I wasn't sure I could live through it. The plane crashed, but I am alive, and I love you more than anything, anything else.'

Francis went still. She lifted her head to run her gaze over the shining black head so close to hers, and when, hidden, he asked so very gently, 'But my love, is it right?' she cried aloud that it was.

He lifted his head and searched her face to find it true. Then, though she felt resplendent already with so much he had given, she was stunned anew as he said with luminosity and wonder, 'I never thought there was a feeling like this. I never knew it existed. Could you come with me and find a new life? I have to tell you in all fairness that you're talking to a man who will shortly be unemployed.'

'*What?*' She looked wild-eyed with the surfeit of shocks dealt to her that day, and he grimaced with recognition of it.

'I quit my job,' he confessed, looking anxious. 'And I didn't mean to tell it to you that way, either. The only thing that I can promise you is that—well, we wouldn't be broke.'

The idiot man—as if she cared, one way or another. Kirstie smoothed his face with both hands, then asked, 'Was it right?'

He could smile. 'The second most right thing I've ever done in my life.'

She looked at him, lean and framed between her fingers, and with her heart in her eyes whispered, 'I could come with you, if you would stay with me. For the rest of tonight.' And with a burst of naked confession, 'Francis, I couldn't let you walk——'

But he would not let her finish. 'You don't have to. Hush. Oh, you know you don't have to. For if you had not offered, I would have begged.'

She wept a little then, for she had been dealt so many blows that day and was weak, and he dried her tears with tenderness and understanding. They sat on the couch, curled as close together as they could get, and after a time she asked, 'Was she so very horrible yesterday?'

Francis gave an angry little laugh and held her closer yet, one hand to her head, as if he were afraid Louise might still be able to do them damage. 'She was not pleasant. But I underestimated the depth of her malice.

I had no idea she would go so far, or hurt you so much.'

Those malignant blue eyes. She shuddered, suddenly chilled and said quietly, 'I think I didn't want to know.'

He stirred. 'Did you know she's the whole reason why you went to Cincinnati in the first place?'

Kirstie lifted her head from his shoulder and searched the softened lines of Francis's face. He looked exhausted, but his eyes were shining clear. 'I don't see how.'

'Simple,' he replied wryly. 'We had that much at least figured out while we waited out that interminable hell for your radio signal. She called Christian and said you wanted to take the flight and spend the weekend in Cincinnati. He was more than happy to have the evening off and saw no reason to question why you would have given her the message to pass on. Paul finally reached him at home with a good blistering, and the whole deception came to light. He came to the airstrip to see if there was anything he could do to help. You know, I like your brothers, though Christian's a bit of a scamp.'

She laughed and buried her face in his shirt, inhaling the delicious scent of him, revelling in the luxury of that precious intimacy. 'That he is, but he's as good as gold, with a soft spot a mile wide.'

'He's certainly protective of you,' Francis said ruefully.

'Oh, dear,' she murmured in dismay, and he caught her hand to fiddle with her fingers. 'What did he say?'

'Well, he was magnanimous enough to admit that he saw possibilities for us, but the general gist was something like, "Break her heart, and I'll break your face."'

She could tell by the line of his cheek that he was smiling, and her hand withdrew from their play to cover her mouth in appalled amusement. 'And what did you say?'

His hand came to tilt up her chin, and he explored with fascination every line and curve of her mobile face. She watched his eyes roam as the smile died, to be replaced by what was still so newborn, it seemed frighteningly fragile. All of it was there for her and she caught her breath.

'I said,' he whispered, 'that to guard your heart was all that I could wish for, as I had already given you mine.'

'Oh, I love you,' she said, and it came from the back of her throat with the force of her feeling, and he thought it the sweetest sound he'd ever heard.

Then his face changed, and hunger, so briefly fed, came back. She quickened inside, with a thrill both of heart and thought, and met his gaze silently with her own. And she took him by the hand to lead him on a slow path up the stairs, dousing the lights one by suspenseful one, until he was a study in moonlit greys like some midnight fantasy.

But this was no fantasy, and it was her bed she was taking him to, the safe haven of warmth and dreams. She opened her door, turned to him and watched her own hand reach out, tentative and seeking. He welcomed it with his own and carried her fingers to his mouth. She stroked his lips. They parted with a sigh, and he turned his face into her open hand to lick her palm. Kirstie's whole body flushed. She started to shake in deep excitement, in impossible panic.

She could feel, as the fingers of her free hand explored his face, that Francis had closed his eyes. He slid his cheek down the forearm, pressed it into the inside of her elbow and whispered, muffled, 'Kirstie. This is stupid. Why am I so afraid?'

The laugh that left her lips sounded more like a sob. When his head came up, she raised herself to her toes, put her arms around his neck and held him tight.

What they spun together was a delicate thing. She introduced him to her nest; he laid her tenderly upon it. Time was passion's labyrinth. They were lost in it together when it collapsed into texture, into the taste of salt and the catch of the breath, the mingling of legs and fingers until there was no future, no doubt, nothing at all but——

'Now,' she murmured, guiding him. He entered her and they made love, and in the passage of that night found joy.

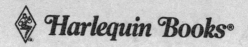

Harlequin Books®

Dear Reader,

Over the past few months, a new schedule for on-sale dates of Harlequin series has been advertised in our books. These dates, however, only apply to the United States. We regret any inconvenience or confusion that may have been caused by this error.

On-sale dates have not changed in Canada, so all your favorite Harlequin series will be available at your local bookstore on their usual dates.

Yours sincerely,

Harlequin Books

Harlequin Superromance®

**Available in Superromance this month
#462—STARLIT PROMISE**

STARLIT PROMISE is a deeply moving story of a
woman coming to terms with her grief and gradually
opening her heart to life and love.

Author Petra Holland sets the scene beautifully, never
allowing her heroine to become mired in self-pity. It
is a story that will touch your heart and leave you
celebrating the strength of the human spirit.

**Available wherever Harlequin books
are sold.**

STARLIT-A